ZANE

ALIEN ADOPTION AGENCY #4

TASHA BLACK

13TH STORY PRESS

13th Story Press

PO Box 506

Swarthmore, PA 19081

13thStoryPress@gmail.com

Cover designed by Sylvia Frost of The Book Brander

ZANE

1

SARAH

Sarah Flynn prided herself on not being easily rattled.

But after a couple of hours aboard a flimsy excuse for a ship, with constant turbulence thrashing her around the cabin and making her bad leg ache, she was starting to question every decision that had brought her here.

Justice, Sarah, she reminded herself firmly. *Justice delayed is justice denied.*

She glanced across the aisle at her fellow adoptive mothers. Each of them was wearing a low-cut purple gown identical to the one Sarah wore. In her opinion, they looked like a trio of floozies headed for certain disaster.

In reality, they were heading to Lachesis, the second moon of the gas-mining planet Hesiod-8, to meet the babies they would adopt and raise.

The women had been recruited by the Alien Adoption Agency back on their respective Terran planets. The intake process was tricky, and very few women made it through.

Unlike most selection processes on the Terras, Sarah had been shocked to realize that the Alien Adoption Agency didn't appear to make its choices based on connections or bribes.

She wasn't really sure how they made their decisions. There had been tests - written, medical and psychological. She hadn't expected to pass, after all, she wasn't exactly doing this because she was longing for a child.

But when she got her letter and arrived at intake along with Liberty and Abigail, there had been no explanation offered for why any of them had been chosen to serve as mothers on Lachesis.

Liberty obviously came from money, but had fallen on low times. Her shoes and clothing were worn when she arrived at intake, but her hair was the striking, iridescent blue-black possible only with expensive in-womb modifications. Whoever her family was, they had raised the elegant Liberty gently. Then perhaps, they had unceremoniously ejected her, leaving her with no option but to flee the planet.

Sarah didn't really know, and she had never asked, since it was none of her business. She had a begrudging respect for Liberty that slowly turned into friendship during their time together.

Abigail, on the other hand, was an open book. They *all* knew *everything* about her six brothers and sisters back home, her old teaching job, her infertility, and the two dozen possible names she had picked out in advance for the baby who would make her a mama. It did no good to remind Abigail that the baby would be Imberian, not Terran, and might not have the same needs and wants as her six younger siblings, whom she had blissfully cared for throughout her childhood. Abigail radiated delight about the whole adoption process.

And much as Sarah hoped the girl wouldn't be disappointed, she couldn't help but feel that Abigail's happiness had smoothed the process for all of them. You couldn't be in her presence without feeling just a little bit light-hearted.

The ship dropped so suddenly that her stomach flipped, and then it caught itself on the air again with a jolt that made her bad leg throb.

Sarah winced and clutched her cane.

She had taken a bullet in that leg during the bank robbery where she lost her father. The surgeons had to take a chunk of muscle from her leg because of the poor quality of the projectile. Now she had a slight limp, and an ache that came and went.

Sarah and her father had run an accounting business and it was tax season on Terra-7 at the time of the robbery. They had been bringing the week's receipts to the bank after a very long day, when an idiot that called himself Jericho Caldwell came marching in, waving an old-fashioned gun around and demanding money.

Banks were insured. All he'd had to do was go up to the counter with a note to be given huge sacks of credits and sent peacefully on his way.

But Caldwell was the kind of man who liked a little drama. So of course things escalated. By the time he made his escape, several people were injured, and Sarah's father was bleeding out on the marble floor.

The city cops hadn't even made a real effort to catch him. They told Sarah there were "bigger fish to fry" and the bank's insurance company would sort it out.

Sure enough, they had paid out a tidy sum. But Reginald Bowen Flynn could not be replaced with a stack of credits. He deserved justice. And if no one would give it to her, then Sarah was determined to hunt down the criminal herself.

She'd begun by hiring a private investigator who had tracked the coward Jericho Caldwell as far as a cargo ship headed for the moon of Lachesis.

But she hit a dead end, because Lachesis was closed to new immigrants, and the PI could follow him no farther.

Sarah had done some homework, and learned that the only legal way onto Lachesis was through a special program, run by the Alien Adoption Agency. All adoptive mothers of Imberian babies would be given land and a modest stipend on one of the moons of Hesiod-8.

It was a long shot, but it was the only shot she had.

So Sarah had walked away from her old life to start this new one. She would begin with justice for her father. After that, she could allow herself to focus on single parenthood on the frontier moon. It was an honorable life, and she hoped to be a good mother, even if she had originally only decided to adopt the child to accomplish her own purposes.

And in her secret heart, she couldn't wait to hold the little one in her arms and lavish it with all the love she had.

"Holy wow," Abigail murmured.

Sarah followed her gaze out the window. The landscape below them looked almost like it was underwater. Low, murky light from between the clouds dappled long, waving grasses. The blues and greens of the vegetation were deeper and more vibrant than back home.

It reminded her of the aquarium her father used to take her to when she was a girl. They would spend hours gazing into the peaceful depths of that underwater world together.

Sarah had just enough time for a pang of quiet happiness to lift her heart at the memory before the ship dropped and caught itself again, causing Liberty to let out an unladylike yelp and then clamp her hand over her own mouth as Abigail giggled.

"*Prepare for landing,*" said a crackly voice over the intercom.

2

ZANE

Zane held the little one securely in his arms. The whelp was very excited and wiggly as he took in the local wildlife.

A school of shiver birds winnowed through the air in formation, their silvery feathers sparkling in the low light. The little one waved his little hands and squeaked as if he wished he could swim after them.

A few feet away, Zane's brother in arms, Rexx, paced with his own whelp, who was still fussy after the landing.

While the men were dragon shifters, whose bodies naturally accommodated environmental changes, the whelps were Imberian, and the lower-than-standard gravity on Lachesis made them uncomfortable.

But Zane was sure Rexx's whelp would adjust to the new gravity soon. The babies had proven very resilient so far.

At the moment, Rexx wore an annoyed expression that had nothing to do with the little one. The blue dragon warrior valued discipline over everything, and the adoptive mothers' ship was late.

"They'll be here soon," Zane said to him, hoping to ease his strain.

"It's not a good sign," Rexx snapped. "What kind of mothers will they be if they can't even be bothered to show up on time for their first meeting?"

"I don't think they're piloting the plane," Zane teased.

He glanced over at Odin, the third member of their group, for back-up. But the red dragon warrior looked even stormier than Rexx.

Odin was never exactly cheerful, but he had been downright snarly ever since the adoption date was scheduled. Zane was pretty sure it had to do with handing over the whelps.

The three were Invicta warriors, each of them with an impressive military career. And their purpose was to protect the younglings, not to form bonds with them.

Long ago, the Invicta had made a terrible mistake, annihilating the gentle people of Imber in an error that would haunt their ranks forever.

The intergalactic counsel had finally given them leave to make things as right as they could. Using preserved DNA from Imber, the Invicta had gestated a group of pod babies who would inherit their planet and its wealth once they were grown.

As part of the deal, each baby would be guarded until the age of twenty standard years by an Invicta warrior. Serving as a guard to an Imberian youth was considered the greatest honor that could be bestowed upon a warrior like Zane.

Some of his brothers took to it more happily than others.

But Zane himself had been both honored and excited to be chosen. He had always liked children. Spending time with a child while also helping to redeem the honor of the Invicta was a dream assignment.

The darker moments of his service seemed like only a memory to him now. Though he tried to approach caring for the whelp with the cool dedication of a professional soldier, it was impossible not to grow fond of its strange sounds and expressions of wonder as it discovered the world all around them. Its warm weight on his chest was a comfort he dared not acknowledge out loud. Zane was a warrior. He should have no need of a whelp to console his heart. His heart should be made of iron.

But it was not. The little one had wrapped a chubby fist around his heart, and it felt like it was made of warm melted chocolate now.

He only hoped that the whelp's new mother would allow him to amuse and nurture the little one when she was busy with other tasks.

If she would not, he supposed the Invicta would still have what they wanted - a soldier willing to give his life to protect a whelp of Imber. A few weeks of unintended bonding had been enough to seal his loyalty forever.

A racket from above distracted him from his thoughts.

"Gods," Rexx murmured. "I hope the adoption agency didn't cut corners in other regards."

Odin made a low, growling sound and wrapped his arms more tightly around his own whelp.

Zane felt sorry for the new mother of that small one.

They all watched as a rickety spacecraft lowered itself nearby, wavy grasses blowing flat under the blast of its thrusters.

A foul-smelling exhaust was spewing from it, and Zane had to fight back the instinct to run for cover with the whelp.

It felt like a trap, like so many of the situations he'd found himself in under active duty on Falnnos. But he had left the dangers of the pirate belt behind in exchange for service on a peaceful frontier. He had to adjust his expectations.

A hatch opened, and workers in bio-suits scrambled out, hastily pitching a decontamination tent.

"Bah," the whelp said in complete surprise, gazing at the flapping tent in wide-eyed wonder.

"That's to make sure no one brings in anything bad for the moon," Zane explained to him.

The whelp chirped like an airlock warning and whacked Zane on top of the head with his little arm.

It was certain that the whelp understood almost nothing that he said. But Zane felt compelled to speak to him anyway. The babes of Imber matured more slowly than dragonets, but one day his words would begin to have meaning for it.

There was a commotion inside the tent and then the flaps flew open to reveal a woman he'd never seen, but who was somehow familiar to him.

She had dark, straight hair and she wore a low-cut swirling gown that was completely at odds with the serious look on her face. She clutched a bag in one hand and something that was either a fighting baton or a walking stick in the other.

As Zane watched, she took two tentative steps, light as a fawn, and her face went soft with wonder.

Something inside him shattered, leaking warmth through his chest until he radiated like a star. From deep within him came one single, unmistakable notion.

Mate...

But that could not be.

Could it?

He watched, gobsmacked, as she marched right up to him, all business now that she had gotten her footing in the slightly lower gravity.

"I'm Sarah," she said, "Sarah Flynn. Is this my son?"

3
___

SARAH

Sarah let her gaze rest on the baby. He had large, intelligent eyes and he was nice and sturdy. He would be a tribute to his grandfather.

But it was suspicious that his skin had the same strange coloration as the man who held him.

"Why is he... yellow?" she asked, holding her arms out. "I thought he was from Imber."

"I am a golden dragon warrior of the Invicta," the man said calmly, without meeting her eyes. "The people of Imber are known to be very adaptable. This whelp is *golden* because he has been in my care. My hue has imprinted on him."

She noticed that he didn't offer her the baby, even though she was clearly holding her hands out.

"Are you with the Alien Adoption Agency?" Sarah asked suspiciously.

"No," he replied, sounding surprised. "I'm the baby's guard."

"I see," Sarah said. "Well, I'm his mother. May I hold him?"

"Of course," he said, meeting her eyes at last.

The intensity of his look nearly caused her to take a step back.

There was something about his bright blue gaze, something almost *familiar*. But that couldn't be. She was certain she'd never met anyone like him before. There was very little need for dragon warriors where she came from.

Pleasure pulsed in her limbs, an unfamiliar sensation. She gulped in a breath of delicious, humid air as she took in other details about the baby's guard.

He was tall, taller than any Terran she'd ever known, and positively rippling with muscles. That golden skin looked rich and lustrous under the cloud cover, and she found herself wondering what he would look like in true sunlight.

But he was holding the baby out now, and she had to cut off those thoughts. She lifted her arms again, feeling tentative this time.

No matter how much she had imagined this moment, she wasn't really ready for it in real life. The responsibility was staggering.

Sarah Flynn had never so much as held a baby before. She had never been all that interested in motherhood, and had no younger siblings.

But as soon as her fingers wrapped around that chubby little body, she instinctively pulled him close.

The baby accommodated himself to her arms, filling in all her empty spaces and warming her, though she hadn't realized she was cold.

He was large, but his weight did not bother her, especially in the reduced gravity. His big blue eyes were serious, in spite of his round, dimpled cheeks, and Sarah felt her soul settle in around him.

"Reginald Bowen Flynn, we are a family now," she told him.

"Who is Reginald Bowen Flynn?" the guard asked, pulling her out of her own little world.

"It's the baby, of course," she shot back at him, angry that he had ruined the moment.

"Isn't that kind of... a long name for a small whelp?" he asked dubiously.

"It was my daddy's name," she retorted. "And he'll grow into it. For now, I'll call him Bowen."

"Bowen," the guard said thoughtfully. "That's nice."

Sarah chose not to reprimand him for his impertinence. What he thought was nice didn't matter. He might be a big hunk of a man used to getting what he wanted by being strong or batting those sexy blue eyes. But the Flynn family wasn't interested in being told what to do, never had been, never would be. And who was a hired guard to judge her actions anyway?

"I think this is our conveyance," he said politely, gesturing to a hover carriage pulled by a large, many-tentacled creature.

"You'll accompany us to our home?" she asked him.

"Of course," he said. "May I carry your bag?"

She nodded. It would be good to have a little help getting settled in.

She tried not to admire the movement of his muscles as he bent to lift her bag and carry it effortlessly to the hover carriage. It was only when they reached the carriage that she remembered to turn back for her friends.

But they were both equally busy attending to their first meetings with their new children. She didn't want to intrude, so she offered them a friendly wave and turned back to the carriage, hoping that one day she would see them again.

Lachesis was vast, but there was always hope. They were three very determined women. She had no doubt they could meet again if they chose to do so.

Bowen let his head rest against her shoulder, and she nuzzled his feathery hair for a moment.

"Are you ready?" the guard asked.

"Of course," she said, rousing herself.

He offered her his hand to help her up. Much as she wanted to refuse it, she had to remember her bad leg and the fact that she was carrying the baby.

When her hand touched his, a sizzle of electricity seemed to sing through her veins, and she let out a little gasp.

He pulled her up quickly, and let go as soon as she had settled into the seat beside him.

But the chorus in her body wouldn't stop its melody, and she snuck a glance at the big golden warrior.

Who had he said he was again? A dragon shifter? That seemed like overkill to accompany a baby for adoption on what was supposed to be a peaceful frontier moon. The only dragon warriors she knew of were the Invicta, and she didn't think it was even possible to hire one of them.

"How long did you say you were with this baby?" she asked.

"I didn't," he said. "I didn't tell you much at all. I've been with the babe a few weeks now. My name is Zane, of the Invicta."

So he *was* Invicta. Incredible. And maybe very lucky for her plans. If he was already here, he might be willing to take on a small side job for her.

"Nice to meet you," she said.

"You as well, Sarah Flynn," he said politely.

She liked that he remembered and repeated her whole name. When she glanced over at him, he winked.

A waterfall of giddiness cascaded over her, and she had to work hard to tamp it down.

Justice, she reminded herself. *Justice and motherhood.*

But the carriage shifted as they rounded a small turn, sending her body closer to his, and she had to fight herself not to think about it.

4

SARAH

Sarah watched the tentacled creature pull the carriage for a long enough time that little Bowen fell asleep on her shoulder. As the sun set over the nearby trees, flickers of colored light illuminated the carriage creature's translucent skin, causing it to sparkle like a holiday light display as it moved them along with its clever tentacles.

"It's a Lachesian octopus," Zane explained. "They're unique to this moon. She's lighting up like that to attract prey."

"Should we stop and feed her?" Sarah asked.

"We're nearly there," Zane said. "No point."

Sarah looked around, but there was no civilization in sight. It occurred to her that there would hardly be suburbs on a frontier moon.

The idea was a lonely one. She had always been a city dweller, the rings of suburbs around New Seattle acting as a buffer between the metal and glass of the city and the barren planes of Terra-7.

The countryside here looked anything but barren. It was

studded with massive trees, with strange mosses floating between them like clouds, all of it so green and blue it looked like a painting.

"Here we are," Zane said, pulling the Lachesian octopus up in front of a strange building in the middle of the trees.

"What is this?" Sarah asked.

"Home," Zane said. "Come on, let's check it out."

She allowed him to help her down, unable to fully brace herself against another shiver of pleasure at his touch.

But she held her sleeping son tight, and set her eyes on the task at hand.

This *home* business was unsettling enough to require her full attention.

From the ground, she could see the same long grasses surrounded the house. It was partially obscured under the canopy of two massive trees, which seemed to be embracing each other over its roof.

Its walls appeared to be made of roughhewn logs, with some sort of concrete crammed between them. This was old-Earth level simplicity, vulnerable to winds, insects, and any man with a strong axe.

At least it was large.

"How many families live here?" she asked Zane, trying to calculate how many apartments it held.

If they had at least one family at each corner, they could possibly defend against prowlers, but not armed ones, not from ground level like that.

And even the thatched wooden roof could be an easy entry point for miscreants with those branches hanging over it. Unless the attic rooms were rented out cheaply to sturdy, working men in exchange for protection. Which she very much doubted with that shallow roofline.

"It's yours," Zane said, sounding confused. "Just yours."

"What do you mean just mine?" she snapped. It had been a long day and she was exhausted. The last thing she wanted was to be put in charge of tenants.

"Come on, I'll show you," he said.

She allowed him to lead her to the door, where she watched suspiciously as he opened it.

The door swung in to reveal a massive space. Beautiful pumpkin-colored wood floors gleamed in the soft sunset that made its way through the trees to stream through the skylights. There was a big stone fireplace, and an assortment of wooden chairs and tables.

Beyond the eating area, she could see a kitchen large to serve a restaurant on Terra-7, with some sort of concrete workspace over the low wood cabinets.

"This is for *one* family?" she asked in wonder.

"Land is cheaper on the frontier," he said. "I take it you're from a city?"

"Land is at a premium where I'm from," she said, nodding. "There would be at least four families in a space like this."

"Shall I show you around?" he offered gruffly.

She nodded and he led the way, pointing to the fireplace as he introduced the *living room*, the big table in the *dining room*, and the various appliances in the kitchen.

"Look good so far?" he asked.

"Seems funny to do your *living* separately from where you cook and eat, but I won't complain," she told him.

She didn't realize she had smiled until he smiled back at her, his blue eyes twinkling. She turned on her heel, pretending to study the shiny new icebox, too embarrassed to let him see the blood rush to her cheeks.

"Do you want to see the bedrooms?" he offered.

"Yes, please," she replied a little too quickly, and then felt the heat in her cheeks all over again at the thought of being alone in a bedroom with the handsome stranger. "Bowen needs his rest," she added.

"He's a good sleeper," Zane agreed. "Come on."

She followed him down a wide hallway until he opened the first door on the left.

"This is Bowen's room," he said.

She peered into the space. It had the same wood floors as the other rooms, but this one had a plush rug on top. It was outfitted with a huge crib, a chair with a rounded sleigh track at its bottom instead of feet, and another door.

"What's through there?" she asked.

"That's a closet," he explained, opening the door to show her what looked like hundreds of baby clothing items.

"My God," she murmured. "He'll grow too fast to wear them all."

"Either way, we'll be ready," Zane said, shrugging.

"We?" she echoed.

"Come on, let's look at your room," he said.

She wanted to ask what kind of mother would ever leave her son in a room with a window *alone*, but she was getting the feeling the lifestyle here was different from back home.

At the end of the hall there was another door, which Zane opened to reveal a spacious bedroom with a plush carpet, massive canopied bed and four windows looking out into the trees.

Sarah stared at it in wonder. It looked like a royal bedroom on a hologram film, not like a place where a real person would sleep.

"Do you like it?" Zane asked quietly.

"I-I can't believe it," she admitted.

"There's a bathroom down the hall," he added. "Let me show you where that is."

She had the sense that he didn't want to embarrass her. Maybe luxurious room sizes were the norm on Ignis-7. But Sarah's family had been solidly middle class, and she had never seen anything like this.

"Here's the bathroom," he said, pointing at a palatial collection of glass tiles and honed concrete with real floating tea lights. "If you want, I can take him so you can freshen up."

"I'm fine," she said. "But don't you have to be going?"

It was nice of him to get her safely to her new house, but she was anxious to be alone and get down to business.

"I'm Bowen's Invicta guard," Zane said sharply. "I'm not going anywhere."

That made sense. The Agency would want to know she was really settled in before leaving her to her own devices. It put a kink in her plans, but she could work around a small delay.

"How long will you be sticking around?" she asked.

"Twenty standard years," he replied matter-of-factly.

Sarah blinked at him, completely shocked, unable to form a reply.

"They didn't tell you?" he asked, less sharply.

She shook her head.

"I'm here to protect the baby," he said. "You'll be glad to have me around."

She looked down the hallway. There was a bedroom, a nursery and a bathroom. In spite of the massive size of the house it seemed unlikely he was really supposed to stay.

"I'll stay in the rocking chair in his room," Zane said, as if reading her mind. "When he gets older, and there's less danger from little things, I can sleep outside."

"Outside?" she echoed stupidly.

"Of course," he said. "I'm a soldier. It's one of my specialties. Also, I'm a dragon, so I don't get cold. I'll keep an eye on you both, to help you and keep you safe."

"You'll help me?" she asked, hitting on an idea of how he could be useful. Well, an idea of how he could be useful that didn't make her blush like a schoolgirl, at least.

"Of course," he said. "Protecting Bowen means making sure you're safe and sound, too. Was there something in particular you were concerned about?"

"So many things," she said, the weight of her relief telling her how worried she had been at tackling a whole new planet without help. "This house is lovely, but it's hardly secure at ground level like this, and with so many points of access."

She looked around, her mind reeling at the potential security risks. There would be time for all that later. Right now, she had more important business.

"But first things first," she announced. "I need to track down the man who killed my father."

"Wow," Zane said, a slightly puzzled look on his face. "I can keep you both safe in this house, no worries there. But the thing about your father sounds... complicated."

"It's not complicated at all," Sarah replied. "My father was an innocent victim at a bank robbery gone wrong. The local police wouldn't chase the villain down, so I did. He's hiding out someplace right here on Lachesis, feeling like he got away with it all, and planning his next score, no doubt. We're going to find him, and take him down, so he can't hurt anyone else."

Zane was silent.

"I'm not asking you out of the goodness of your heart," she added. "I'll pay you good money."

5

ZANE

Zane stared down at the little Terran, unable to believe what he had just heard.

It was bad enough that this sweet-looking woman had just told him she wanted to kill someone.

But now she wanted to *pay him* to help her do it...

And all the while, the mate bond thrummed between them, driving him nearly insane with its insistence.

"No, Sarah," he said at last. "Absolutely not. What you're talking about is murder."

"What he did to my father was murder," she said in an affronted way. "I want to make sure he doesn't do it to someone else's family member."

"Then we'll bring him to the law," Zane told her.

"It doesn't work that way. I told you, I already tried." she said, looking exasperated. "They didn't even care back on Terra-7, where the crime was committed. Why would they do anything here?"

"You won't know for sure that they won't help unless you ask them," he suggested, hating to admit that she was probably right. "We'll just keep making noise until they listen."

"Aren't you a solider?" she demanded. "Haven't you killed people?"

"Of course," he told her, trying not to let the memory sear him all over again. "But it was never for money. It was only to protect my homeland."

"So fighting for your family is okay, but not for mine?" she asked.

"There's a difference between facing a man on a battlefield and hunting him down like a dog," Zane said.

"Jericho Caldwell *is* a dog," Sarah said, her voice low and intense. "He killed my father in cold blood, and I'm going to bring him to justice. With or without your help."

"You're not talking about justice, Sarah," Zane told her, running a hand through his hair. "You're talking about revenge."

"I don't see a difference," she said, her voice going up a note in frustration.

Zane winced, but it was too late, Bowen had awoken on her shoulder. He let out a mewling cry.

Bowen didn't like arguments or loud sounds. He was a sensitive soul, and he craved peace and routine, neither of which he was getting right now.

Sarah looked down at the baby in surprise, as if she had forgotten he existed. It hit Zane that she wasn't here for Bowen. Bowen was just her ticket to Lachesis, her key to hot-headed revenge.

She probably didn't care about the whelp at all.

Fury rose in his chest at the thought.

"I'll take him," he offered, putting out his arms and willing himself to stay calm, though he could feel the dragon's wings rustling in his shoulder blades.

She looked back and forth between him and the baby for a moment, then handed the little one over. Zane held the baby protectively to his chest and watched Sarah smooth back her already smooth hair.

As soon as she was finished with her hair, she marched for the door, her cane made an annoying, self-satisfied tap with every step.

He was furious to feel a tug on his soul, as if the mate bond *compelled* him to follow her into certain trouble.

She is not my mate, he told himself as he followed. *I'm just keeping her out of danger until I can talk some sense into her.*

But the dragon in his chest shivered with delight. He was not bothered by his mate's bloodthirsty tendencies. Far from it.

The dragon liked that she was ferocious in the name of her family. The words of righteous fury she spoke were a language he knew all too well, and he growled and crooned along to the rhythm of her angry strides like they were music.

Where she led, he would always follow.

6

SARAH

Sarah headed out the door, wondering how she could stop to ask Zane about feeding the Lachesian octopus without letting go of her anger.

But as soon as she reached the lawn in front of the house, she could see that the creature had already taken care of its own needs. Six of its tentacles were hugging the remains of something too far gone to struggle, as the other two shoved it into the octopus's beaky maw.

By the time Sarah neared her, there was no sign that the octopus had been eating at all. Except that she wasn't glowing like she had swallowed a string of holiday lights anymore.

"Don't approach her from the front," Zane's deep voice called out from the doorway.

"Why not?" Sarah asked, turning back to see him striding toward her with Bowen on his hip.

"She just ate, and sometimes they eject part of the prey if they can't digest it," he told her. "Go on, take the whelp and get into the carriage. I'll harness her."

Sarah took Bowen from Zane and headed for the

carriage. She was dying to ask Zane if he was coming with her after all to help her track Caldwell. He hadn't had much time for a change of heart, but she could always hope.

Bowen was so warm and sleepy. He snuggled against her chest as if he forgave her for upsetting him earlier.

She felt a wave of gratitude that almost brought tears to her eyes.

"I'm sorry, Bowen," she whispered to him. "I'll try to do better."

Zane had the octopus harnessed again in no time, and swung himself up into the carriage beside her.

"Giddyap," he told the creature.

The carriage began to roll behind the half-floating octopus.

"What time is it?" Sarah wondered out loud.

"Early evening," Zane told her.

"I thought it was early evening when my ship landed," she said.

"That's the cloud cover," Zane said. "You'll get used to it. Some people say it's romantic."

Sarah looked out over the murky landscape. "Seems more foreboding than romantic."

Zane nodded, but it looked like he was trying not to smile.

"What?" she asked.

"You're so serious," he told her. "I'm not used to it."

"You think women should have heads full of spun sugar?" she asked. Seemed about right that a big lug like this one would hang around a bunch of giddy women.

"Not at all," he said. "I spend most of my time with the other warriors."

"You expect me to believe that Invicta warriors spend all their time giggling like schoolgirls?" she asked.

"Well not when you put it that way," he said, sounding a little affronted. "But when you're in the trenches, it's best to have a sense of humor."

She nodded.

"Sarah," he said gently. "Parenthood is going to be a long road. I've only known your son a few weeks and it's already changed me. It might help if you lighten up your outlook a little. Focus on Bowen."

"You aren't going to help me," she said, hating that her voice broke and gave him a glimpse of the tears she was struggling to contain.

"Sarah," he said.

"I thought you changed your mind when you came out here," she said. "I thought you were coming with me to help me find Caldwell."

The despair threatened to overwhelm her, and she had to focus on her breathing, just like in the first days after the bank.

"I didn't change my mind, but I am coming to help you," he said. "I'm not going to kill anyone. I'm just going to try to keep you safe."

She wanted to scream at him, but she buttoned her lip. She had just promised the baby she would try not to upset him again and she wasn't going to begin motherhood by going back on her word.

Instead of continuing the conversation, she looked out over the countryside as they traveled.

Now that she was really looking, she could see there were other dwellings hidden among the trees and carved into the hillsides.

"Are those cave houses?" she asked Zane without meaning to.

"They're called dugouts," he explained. "It's a simple

way to make a frontier home without having to chop down trees."

"Wouldn't it be cold in there?" Sarah asked.

"They use blocks made of sod for the part that isn't in the hillside," Zane explained. "The soil insulates, and there's usually venting for a fire pit."

Sarah nodded, taking it in. It was strange to see a regular aluminum plated door on a wall made of earth, but the frontier was a difficult place if you were low on funds. Why not let the mountain provide shelter?

"Do you feel lucky to have such a nice house?" he asked. "Puts it in a whole new perspective, doesn't it?"

"I can't believe that giant house is mine," Sarah agreed. "But it won't stay that way if we don't work on our security."

"I'm a dragon warrior," Zane pointed out.

"But there's only one of you," she replied firmly.

The country around them had begun to give way to a small town. It had a large open plaza with posts to tie up carriage animals. Large clay-brick buildings with some sort of bound grass roofing lined the street.

There was a general store, a saloon, a bank and then a building that looked completely out of place.

"What's that?" she asked, pointing at the dome-shaped edifice at the center of town that looked to be made of some kind of graphene-laced polymer. It would have stood out as far too high-tech for the city she was from. Out here, it was like seeing a dog wearing a diamond tiara.

"Oh, that's the courthouse," Zane told her. "It was shipped in from Athena's Belt in prefabricated pieces. The founder of the Lachesis colony was a big fan of Old Athena's Belt architecture, so he had it brought in and assembled. The other buildings are made of local materials. That fluffy looking roofing on all the stores is the same floating moss we have in the trees back at home."

Home.

It was funny to think of that gigantic log building as her home - *their* home. But Sarah felt an odd pang of longing at the idea.

Zane pulled up the carriage and tied it to a post, then offered Sarah his hand. She took it and felt the rush of awareness that happened every time they touched.

"Do you want me to take him so it's easier for you with the cane?" Zane offered.

It was only then that she realized she had hopped out of the carriage without her cane, and she hadn't even noticed.

"I-I don't think I need it," she said wonderingly.

"The lower gravity helps a lot of people with joint pain," Zane said. "Should we bring it anyway, in case you get tired?"

"Sure," she said. "Thank you."

He leaned past her and plucked the cane from the carriage floor.

It was impossible not to notice his size, his delicious scent, and even the warmth that seemed to pour off him.

She wondered what it would feel like to run her open palms down his chest.

He straightened and she could see his blue irises flash gold for a moment, as if the dragon had been peering out at her through his eyes.

Somehow, the idea was thrilling rather than frightening. Blood rushed to her cheeks and she pressed her lips to Bowen's fluffy head and closed her eyes to focus herself.

He's a guard. And he's not here for me. He's here for Bowen. We both are.

"Excuse me, my lord," a man's voice said.

She opened her eyes and turned to see a middle-aged man in a beautiful Myrrish suit waiving a brochure in their direction.

"I hope you won't think me presumptuous," the man said, his eyes twinkling under a wide brimmed hat. "But I can see by the carriage, and the cut of your wife's gown, that you are a man of taste."

Sarah wanted to grab him by the collar and ask him what her ridiculous dress had to do with her husband's taste. But Zane wasn't even her husband, and the man was obviously just talking nonsense because he was selling something.

"What's this?" Zane asked, nodding at the brochure without taking it.

"I can see you are a gentleman who gets right down to business," the man exclaimed. "I like that. Now, this, this..."

He gazed down fondly at the brochure, as if it were a child or a favorite pet and he was at a loss for words to describe it.

"It's the best value in the sector," he said suddenly, looking up at them. "Maybe the whole system."

"It looks like a brochure," Sarah snapped. It had been a long day, too long for all this.

"It is, my dear," the man said. "This is the description and layout of Lachesis Valley, a development of exceptional homes for exceptional owners, located in the gravity-light valley of Lachesis moon."

"A housing development?" Sarah echoed. "People here are living in log cabins and dugouts."

"Some people are," the man said with just the tiniest air of snobbishness. "But people like you and your husband don't have to. I see you came to Lachesis because of your infirmity." He nodded at her cane. "The Valley offers four different models, each with one-story living and absolutely no stairs needed. My guarantee to all my customers is that your new home in the Valley will allow you the comforts you need to live as if you were young and whole."

Young and whole?

"I took a bullet in the leg trying to save my daddy from a bank robber," Sarah spluttered.

"That was very brave of you," the man allowed, looking a little shocked. "A daughter like that deserves to live in style and comfort," he recovered quickly.

"We'll think about it," Zane said, grabbing the brochure and trying to steer Sarah away.

If she hadn't been holding Bowen she would have been sorely tempted to yell at the man. How dare he accuse people of not being *whole* just because they needed a cane?

"You'll want to decide quickly," the man said, holding onto the brochure in an attempt to keep them in his thrall. "When Lachesis reopens immigration to off-mooners again, you won't be able to get a spot on my waitlist for love or money. Right now, I have a special where I'm waiving the lot premiums on two of my best sites."

"Thank you," Zane said firmly.

The man let go of the brochure and they started off.

"Come by and visit my model homes any time, little lady," he called after them. "Ask for Moar Talfox."

Sarah didn't look back.

The plaza around them was bustling with life. Just ahead of them, a line of people and droids stood in the brick dust. Some were chatting and playing some sort of game with bottle caps, others just stood, looking around hopefully.

A cart drove up and the driver shouted something. Two men and a duster droid hopped in, and then it drove off.

"What was that about?" Sarah asked.

"They're hired hands, waiting for work," Zane explained. "Most of them are saving up for their own farms. Lachesis is a place where you can get a fresh start at any age."

"So, they just stand here in the plaza most of the day waiting?" Sarah asked.

"Unless they get hired," Zane said.

"Excellent," Sarah replied, heading straight over to the men.

7

———

ZANE

Zane watched in awe as Sarah marched straight up to the line of men, Bowen still on her hip.

"Excuse me, gentlemen," she said in a crisp, bell-like voice.

Everyone turned to her, a few wrinkled faces broke into smiles at the sight of little Bowen.

"I'm looking for someone," Sarah said. "He goes by the name of Jericho Caldwell back on Terra-7, but he might have another name here. He's a tall, skinny man and he's missing the ring finger on his left hand. He would be a bit of a newcomer, like me."

Suddenly, shoes were shuffled and droids began whirring into their back-up programs. No one would make eye-contact with Sarah.

"He's no good," she went on, a note of despair in her voice. "He killed my father in cold blood, and he'll get up to mischief here too. Does anyone remember seeing someone who fits his description? I'll pay good money for information that leads to his capture."

She waited long enough, looking up and down the line, that Zane felt embarrassed for her.

But there were no takers.

She turned on her heel at last and headed back to him.

"Why won't anyone help?" she demanded. "Doesn't anyone here care?"

Bowen's eyes went wide, and he squeaked and waved his little hand as if he also wanted answers.

"Come on, let's keep walking," Zane said in what he hoped was a calming way. "I'll do my best to explain on the way."

She set her chin, but she started walking with him.

"A lot of people come to a new moon to get away from things that happened in their old lives," Zane said carefully. "It's tough to ask a man to turn in another when they both have their demons."

"He *killed my father*," Sarah said. "Am I supposed to believe the Alien Adoption Agency sent me to a moon full of murderers to raise this boy?"

"I'm just saying that people may not want to get involved," Zane said. "You just got here. They don't really know him, or you. Maybe give it a little time?"

But Sarah caught sight of something else, and she was already marching off.

Zane glanced up at the facade of the building she was approaching. The saloon.

He sighed and followed her, the string between his heart and hers already pulled too tight. He stepped into the large, open room, dim, even compared to the overcast sky outside.

"You can't bring a baby in here," the matron said, scowling at Sarah as she approached the bar.

"Darned skippy I can," Sarah replied. "Don't worry. He won't start any trouble."

The woman barked out a laugh and stepped aside, apparently Zane wasn't the only one who could see there was no point arguing with the feisty little Terran.

"Keep her out of trouble," the matron muttered as Zane followed Sarah.

"Yes, madam," he muttered back, wondering how exactly she thought he was going to do that.

The saloon was thick with strange smoke and the mingled scent of sweat and belt grease.

Workers, droids, and even a few merchants sat at small wooden tables. Many were eating bowls of a steaming stew and sloshing wooden cups of sweet-smelling brew as they talked.

He caught up to Sarah as she reached the bar. She had found them two stools at the center, between groups of grizzled patrons.

"This might not be the best place to start," he told her quietly.

"Nonsense," she replied. "A no-good miscreant like Jericho Caldwell would hightail it to the saloon first thing after landing. We'll get to the bottom of things quickly here. *If anyone here is man enough to share what he knows.*"

She said the last part loudly enough for their seat mates at the bar to hear it. One or two turned around and treated them to a display of dirty faces and neglected dental hygiene.

"Hello, neighbors," Sarah said, before Zane could beg her to stop. "My name is Sarah Flynn, and I'm looking for the man who killed my father. His name is Jericho Caldwell. He looks like a rat, but with more fleas, and he's missing the ring finger of his left hand."

She paused for a moment and took in the murmurings.

"I'm prepared to offer a reward for information that leads to his capture," she went on.

The room went quiet, but no one approached.

"I'll be here at the bar, if you change your minds," she said, undaunted, and turned back to Zane.

"There," she said, with satisfaction. "Now we wait."

Zane was pretty sure she could wait here until the local sun went supernova, and no one was going to give her one byte of information, but he hated to break her good mood.

"Shall we have a drink?" he offered.

She looked torn, but she nodded and sat down on one of the stools.

Bowen was wide awake, looking around at the other patrons with his large blue eyes.

"Hey there, little feller," the woman behind the bar said, resting her cyborg arm on the counter to smile at him.

Bowen squeaked at her and then hid his little face in Sarah's neck.

"How old is he?" the barkeep asked.

Sarah glanced up at Zane in a panic. Gods above, she didn't even know the baby's age.

"He's just old enough that we're too sleep deprived to remember," Zane joked weakly.

The barkeep slapped her towel against the bar and hooted. "D'ja hear that, Evarn?" she asked one of the old timers next to them at the bar.

"I heard it," he said, tipping his visor.

"What can I get you two?" the barkeep asked.

"Surprise us," Zane said.

"But not with strong spirits," Sarah added.

"Coming right up," the woman agreed.

"Your name is Evarn?" Sarah asked the man beside her.

"Yes, miss," he said.

"That's lovely," she told him. "I know people here seem to keep to themselves, but you don't know anything about the man I asked about, do you?"

"Don't mention that bastard's name around here," Evarn hissed.

"He did come to town," the barkeep murmured, setting down two steaming wooden mugs in front of them. "Like you said, he's no good, you can smell it on him."

"Bad tipper, eh, Rose?" Evarn asked with a wink.

"Now that you mention it, yes," she said. "Anyway, he was going by Jay Caldwell, missing that finger though, just like you said. He started doing jobs for the Sons of Sirius."

"The who?" Sarah asked.

"Hoverbike gang out of Hesiod 8," Evarn explained.

"He had a falling out with them over a girl," Rose confided. "Started something up with the leader's woman is what I heard. Then lit out for the unclaimed territories when it got too hot around here."

"Interesting," Sarah noted.

"He's not harming no one," the man beside Zane said suddenly. "You let him be."

"Too late," Sarah said. "He's harmed someone already. Let's go, Zane."

She slid off the stool, but before she could head for the door, Bowen let out a sad little cry.

"Oh no, baby, what's wrong?" she asked.

Bowen banged his head on her shoulder.

"He's hungry," Zane told her. "We should get him some milk."

"You look like you could all use a meal," Rose said. "Why don't you take that table. I'll bring you a good dinner. Then you can decide what to do." Rose pointed to a well-lit booth by the window.

Sarah looked torn.

"Please," Zane said softly. "She's right. We could all use a meal."

Bowen bumped her shoulder with his head again and Sarah nodded to the barkeep.

"Thank you, Rose," she said. "We would be much obliged."

Relief flooded through Zane as they headed to the table.

A man at the table next to theirs gazed at Sarah with a thoughtful expression. He was different from the other men in the saloon - younger, sharper, and clean-shaven.

Zane disliked him immediately.

8

SARAH

Sarah sat back in the wooden booth with Bowen on her lap.

The baby slapped his small hands on the table and made growling sounds.

"He knows it's dinner time," she said, delighted.

Zane was looking at the next table, a stern expression on his handsome face.

She followed his gaze to see a man seated by himself.

The man stood out in the smoky saloon for being neat and clean. He had well-kept dark hair to his shoulders and wore a handsome gray uniform.

He nodded to her when he noticed her looking, his eyes bright with interest.

She nodded back, wondering what he might want. She doubted a decent man would know anything about Jericho Caldwell, but she wouldn't close the door on any conversation that might lead to help.

"Madam," the man said, then nodded to Zane. "And my lord. May I have a word?"

"By all means," Zane said, indicating their table.

But Sarah noticed Zane was still scowling. She had no idea why. The man seemed nice enough to her.

The stranger rose from his own table, and took a seat across from Sarah.

Zane seated himself beside Sarah.

She could feel the heat of his muscular thigh through his breeches and her gown, and the sensation made her almost lightheaded. She pushed the thoughts aside and tried to focus on business.

"What can we do for you?" Zane asked.

The stranger clasped his hands together and placed them on the table, gazing directly into Sarah's face.

She could see now that his eyes were slate gray, as if his uniform had been purposely dyed to match them.

"I'm a marshal," he told her. "Name's Booker Slade, but everyone just calls me Slade."

"Sarah Flynn," she replied. "My son, Reginald Bowen Flynn, and his guard, Zane of the Invicta."

She felt Zane flinch beside her as if she had slapped him and wondered if he hadn't wanted his name shared for some reason.

"Pleasure," the man called Slade said, eyebrows slightly lifted as he observed Zane.

These men and their pissing contests.

So one was a dragon warrior, and one was a marshal, so what? Her father was still dead, and no one was hunting the killer. So they were both about as useless as a harvester droid at a canning factory.

"Will the marshals help us hunt down Caldwell and bring him to justice?" she asked plainly.

"No, ma'am," Slade replied, a touch of sorrow in those kitten-gray eyes. "But I will."

Rose appeared with two bowls of food, a basket of bread and a pitcher of milk as well as a stack of wooden glasses.

Bowen began fussing immediately, as if the sight of his milk and bread had caused him to panic instead of take comfort.

"Dip a bit of bread in the milk for him," Zane suggested quietly. "If it's nice and soft he'll be happy with it."

She did as he suggested, and soon Bowen was eating bits of bread as fast as she could wet them.

A few quiet minutes passed as they ate, and finally the baby slowed down and rested against her chest.

"So," Sarah said, glancing up at Slade.

"So?" he echoed.

"Why would you help me?" she asked. "You don't look like you're hurting for money. And you say the marshals won't help officially."

"They won't, because they think they have better things to do," he said. "I will, because I've got my eye on a sweet piece of farmland and I'm looking for a side gig so I can get my hands on it. How big a reward are you talking about?"

"Not as big as all that," Sarah said. "But it won't be such a big job either. We already know he's hiding out in the territories. It should be easy."

Slade chuckled and took a sip of his drink.

"What?" Sarah asked.

"The territories are far from easy," Slade said. "Full of dangerous animals and people who don't want to be found. And there's no shortage of places to hole up. Knowing that he's there doesn't narrow things down as much as you'd think."

"I thought you were an intergalactic marshal," Sarah said. Goading him a little couldn't hurt.

"I am," he said.

"But you're afraid of some space crocodiles and a few petty criminals?" she asked.

Zane roared with laughter beside her.

"Your husband is an Invicta dragon warrior, and I don't see him trotting over there," Slade said, narrowing his eyes at Zane.

"He's not my husband," she said, feeling a little pang at the words and then hating herself for it. "And he doesn't believe in justice."

"I don't believe in revenge," Zane barked. "They're two different things."

"Not this time they're not," she spat back.

"Sweetheart, the Invicta are different from you and me," Slade said in a honeyed tone.

"Don't *sweetheart* me," Sarah said, turning her fury on the stranger. "This job is worth two thousand credits to me, no more, no less. Either take it or don't. I'll have no more arguments in front of my boy."

"Two thousand credits," he sputtered.

"Take it or leave it."

He narrowed his eyes at her.

She focused on breathing slow and even, without lowering her eyes from his, or even blinking.

Sarah had only two thousand one hundred seventy credits to her name. She had left the rest to provide for her mother.

Two thousand credits was more than fair pay for a few days' work for the marshal. And she needed the one hundred seventy to tide them over until Bowen's stipend arrived.

Slade sucked in a breath and appeared to make a decision.

"I'll do it," he said. "But only because I have a soft spot for pretty single mothers."

Zane stiffened beside her.

"I don't care why you do it," Sarah said. "We'll meet you at the road out of town at dawn, Mr. Slade."

9

———

SARAH

Sarah found herself nodding off on the ride home.

It was dark, and Bowen was sleeping already, his warm weight curled against her chest. Her belly was full, and the carriage jostled lightly.

Between those comforts and the absence of pain in her leg, Sarah felt like she was floating.

Zane drove on in silence, his eyes on the path ahead and the Lachesian octopus, which was glowing a pale rainbow of color again.

"She's hungry," Sarah said dreamily, happy that there was something about this strange new moon that she recognized.

"We'll release her again when we get home," Zane said. "She'll be able to catch more than enough to satisfy herself now that it's full night."

"Thank you," Sarah said.

"For what?" he asked.

"I know you didn't want to take me out," she said. "But I'll rest easy when I know Caldwell can't hurt anyone else."

He nodded, and looked out into the night.

There was something about his expression, something almost haunted. She wondered what could make such a fearsome warrior look so lost.

But before she came up with any hypotheses, he pulled the octopus up.

They were home again.

Home.

How did it sound so foreign and so completely right at the same time?

Zane swung down and released the octopus, as promised. It half floated, half tiptoed into the trees, looking delirious with happiness, internal lights flickering in a wild rainbow.

Zane came back and held out his arms for Bowen.

Sarah handed him down and was amazed to see Zane cuddle the little one into his chest quickly enough that he didn't wake.

"Now you," he said, offering Sarah his hand.

She took it, anticipating the shiver this time, but still not ready for it to travel down her spine and warm her cheeks.

When she touched down on the ground he didn't back up. Instead he stood frozen pinning her between the carriage and his big, hard body.

"Sarah," he breathed.

She lifted her chin, daring herself to look into those bright blue eyes. Something was happening between them. Something primal and true and good.

Before her eyes reached his, she sensed movement in the shadows.

Instantly, the hair at the back of her neck lifted up and her heart began to pound.

"What's that?" she whispered to Zane, gazing out into the trees.

He turned, quick as a thought, putting his body between hers and the danger she had spotted.

She was just able to see an ominous shadow stretching toward them before he fully blocked her view of the house. Now that the two of them had gone silent she could hear voices coming from that direction as well.

"Are you sure they're not home?" one voice whispered.

"Does it look like anyone's home?" another hissed.

Sarah peeked out from behind Zane's back to see the shadow stretch further, lifting a large object to break in the door.

"Hold him, please," Zane whispered.

Sarah took Bowen and snuggled him close.

By the time she looked up from settling him in, Zane was gone.

In his place was a massive golden dragon, shimmering in the dim light of the stars through the haze of clouds.

He lit up like the sun, illuminating the clearing in front of the house and revealing every detail, every leaf on the trees above, each axe mark in the logs that made up the house.

Sarah's mouth dropped open as she took in the ocean of exquisite golden scales and the sheer size of the beast before her. She should have been afraid. She should have been *terrified*.

But somehow, she had never felt safer in her life.

"*Ha*," Bowen yelled sleepily to the dragon.

Someone gasped.

Sarah turned to see a very surprised looking couple standing in front of the door to her house.

The man was holding a note that he had been about to affix to her door.

The woman was holding a cake, but she seemed to have

forgotten about it in her shock over the appearance of the dragon. As she stared in open wonder at Zane, the cake was very slowly sliding off the plate.

It landed with a splat on the doorstep.

"Hello," the man called out.

"Oh dear," the woman said, crouching to pick up the cake.

The air around the magnificent dragon seemed to waver for a moment and then it was gone, and Zane stood in its place once more.

"Sorry to scare you," he called back to them.

"We're sorry if we looked suspicious," the man said, striding up. "We just wanted to welcome you. We live down the road a piece."

Zane smiled and offered the man his arm.

Timidly, the man took it and they clasped.

"Pleasure is ours," Zane said to him. "Again, sorry for the scare."

Sarah couldn't begin to understand why the neighbors would be sneaking around in the night. They were lucky Zane hadn't taken them both out. But she kept her mouth shut. There was no point scolding them now. They looked scared enough that she doubted they'd try to welcome any more neighbors in the night.

"So sorry, dear," the woman said from where she stood on the doorstep. "If you'll just lend me a rag, I'll clean this up and we'll bring you another tomorrow."

She looked terrified. Like Zane might change his mind at any moment and decide to eat them as a snack instead of the cake.

"Please, don't trouble yourself," Sarah said. "If you'd like to come in, I'll take care of that."

The couple exchanged nervous glances.

"No thank you," the woman said quickly. "We have to be going. We'll see you another time. Again, our apologies."

They scurried back down the country lane before anyone had a chance to object.

Zane joined Sarah by the doorstep, and they looked down at the cake.

It was perfect except for the fact that it was sitting on the ground. The frosting glistened in the starlight.

"That actually looks really good," Zane said.

"Are you thinking what I'm thinking?" Sarah asked.

10

ZANE

Zane stood at the kitchen counter ten minutes later, a big plate of cake in front of him, watching Sarah try to eat hers neatly while Bowen snatched for it.

"I can't believe you sliced the bottom right off without ruining the frosting on the top," he said wonderingly. "You're very good with a knife."

"We're just lucky she dropped it the way she did," Sarah said, nodding sagely.

Her mouth was a little full and she had frosting on her chin, which Bowen was trying to scoop off with his little fingers.

Zane could hardly blame him. The cake was delicious - a slab of moist, buttery goodness, with fluffy frosting and a layer of some kind of cream on the inside.

"Did you want some frosting, baby?" Sarah asked him.

Bowen let out a string of excited syllables in response.

Zane watched as Sarah dipped his little hand into her slice of cake.

The expression of wonder on the whelp's face was priceless when his hand went into his mouth.

"Good, right?" Sarah asked him. "Maybe having the neighbors stop by wasn't such a bad thing."

"That really scared you," Zane remembered out loud.

"Didn't it scare you?" she replied.

"Not really," he admitted. "I didn't like the idea of someone prowling around our house, but I get the feeling you were really frightened."

"First of all, I can't turn into a spaceship sized reptile when there's a prowler," Sarah said. "And yes, I was terrified, at first. We're really exposed out here."

"You were worried earlier about keeping the house safe," Zane said. "Now that you've seen me as a dragon, do you feel better?"

"Fishing for compliments, eh?" she teased, licking frosting off her finger.

His heart almost stopped beating at the sight of that sweet pink tongue darting out to caress her hand. He gulped and shook his head to clear it.

"Not at all," he told her. "I want you to feel safe. If seeing me shift didn't do it, then tell me what will."

"Seeing you shift was incredible," she admitted. "You were... beautiful and terrifying."

The dragon preened in his chest as he waited for her to tell him why it wasn't enough.

"But you have to sleep sometime," she said. "What happens to Bowen and me in the night when you're asleep and someone pries open a window?"

The thought chilled his blood, even as he knew that the dragon's senses would wake him instantly if their family was in danger.

"What if I secure the doors and windows tonight?" he offered. "We can figure out something more permanent tomorrow. But for now, would you sleep better if I made sure no one could open a door or window without waking me?"

Her eyes went soft, and she nodded up at him.

Bowen was resting his round cheek against her chest again. It was probably time for the little one to get some rest.

Zane tried to convince himself he wasn't just trying to get the baby out of her arms so he could find his own way into them.

"Let me get the window Bowen's room first, so you can put him down when he's ready," he said, jogging off for the nursery.

The baby's room was peaceful. Zane drank in the sight of the crib and rocker.

Though he was only supposed to guard the whelp, it was impossible not to love him. Seeing this cozy space where Bowen would spend his nights made Zane feel a contentment that he could not have explained before knowing the little one.

By the time he was finished securing the window, Sarah was heading down the hallway with a clean and sleepy Bowen.

Zane backed up to the wall to let her pass and tried not to notice her incredible scent as that low-cut gown slid against his thigh.

Why was she wearing it? She was one of the most practical people he had ever met. It seemed completely out of place.

But the small, fierce Terran was a mystery to him.

He watched her bend over the crib and lower Bowen in.

The little one began to fuss, but she reached in and stroked his belly, instinctively knowing what would comfort him.

Zane forced himself away from the doorway. There were

plenty of windows and doors. If he wanted to be able to reassure her that all were firmly locked and secured, he had to get to work.

But when he reached her bedroom he had to stop again.

Behind him, back in Bowen's room, Sarah had begun to sing. Her rich, contralto voice was soft and comforting in the still night of the darkened house.

Bowen settled right away, as if he wanted to hear her voice as badly as Zane did.

The song was nonsense, a list of gifts a parent promised a child in exchange for going to sleep. But the melody unlocked something in his chest, and he felt like he was falling.

She wants to kill someone, he reminded himself. *She isn't as sweet as she seems.*

But he knew her better now. He understood her feelings for her father, and her fears about what could happen to her son.

Even if he knew killing a man was not the answer, he could see why she would want to attempt it. She wanted to keep her family safe.

And then a cloak of sadness fell over him.

Sarah Flynn was a determined woman. If she wanted that man dead, he was pretty sure she could make it happen.

And if she got her wish, she would have to live with the consequences.

Zane had trained since he was a fledgling to be prepared for war and death. But he was still haunted by the things he had done.

The big-hearted woman singing in the room next door was not equipped to deal with the knowledge that she had ended a life. He knew to his bones she was not.

How long until his sweet Sarah was a ghost of herself,

wandering this house, wishing she could undo what she had done?

I could distract her. I could make her forget what she came here to do.

The idea stopped him in his tracks.

It was the height of vanity to think he could seduce her into letting go of her plans, but he knew the effect he had on women, and on this woman in particular. He had clocked his effect on Sarah with the dragon's superior senses. When he was close her pulse quickened and the blood rushed to her cheeks.

Mate, the dragon groaned in his head.

But if he claimed her, and allowed the mate bond to draw them together permanently, he could not imagine the suffering they both would feel if she did not give up her quest for revenge.

Mate.

The dragon's voice was insistent.

And the beast was right. It was too late for Zane to resist her. The delicate bond already held him fast like a spider's web, soft and smooth as silk until he tried to pull away.

He was hers, and she was his.

The sooner she knew it, the better.

11

SARAH

Sarah gazed down at the peaceful face of her son.

He was asleep already, so there was no need for her to keep patting his little belly.

But there was something so sweet about communing quietly here with him.

His cheeks were pillowy soft, and his lower lip pouted in his sleep. He looked like one of the cherubs from the books her grandmother had read to her in her childhood, except for his beautiful golden skin.

Being his mother would be the greatest joy and responsibility of her life. She had hoped to bond with the baby, but she never dreamed it could be so easy, that she could love him so fiercely after only a few hours.

She tried to picture him older, and herself even more besotted.

"He's amazing, isn't he?" Zane's low voice roused her from her dreams.

She turned to find him standing close behind her, gazing into the crib with a soft expression. She wondered if that was what she looked like, watching Bowen sleep.

"You love him too," she realized out loud.

"My job is to protect him," the warrior said gruffly.

"You do protect him," Sarah said. "But you also love him."

Zane's eyes went to hers and she felt a flash of recognition go through her.

This wasn't the first time today she had felt it. She was attracted to him, of course, he was incredibly handsome. Who wouldn't be?

But it wasn't just desire she felt. It was sense of the familiar. A sense of *home*.

"Sarah," he said softly.

She reached for him in spite of herself, needing to touch that tense jaw.

He held perfectly still as she stroked his cheek.

The world pulled in tightly until there was nothing but the sensation of his rough jaw under her hand and the taut pull of his blue eyes.

Suddenly, she was being lifted up.

Zane cradled her in his warm arms, heading for her bedroom with a purposeful stride.

"Wh-what are we doing?" she murmured without taking her hand from his face.

But he carried her into her room and shut the door behind them without replying.

She closed her eyes, drinking in the sensations. His arms were so strong, the planes of his chest so firm, that she felt like she was floating in an ocean of masculinity.

He set her down on the edge of the bed and knelt at her feet.

"Do you feel it?" he asked.

She swore she could hear the harmonics in his voice, feel the pull of his desire for her.

"Yes," she whispered.

"Do you know what it means?" His voice was raspy and low.

She didn't know. But she felt a longing so low and sweet she thought she might die.

"You are my mate," he told her. "And the bond between us is already tightening, though I haven't claimed you yet."

Mate?

She blinked and tried to come out of the trance he had her in.

"Dragons know our mates from the moment we meet. And we mate for life," he told her. "I know we just met, but we have the rest of our lives to get to know each other."

"For life?" she managed to echo.

"Yes," he said simply. "I'm not like Terran men, Sarah. When I claim you, it will be forever."

She tried to take it in, and couldn't. All she wanted was for him to touch her.

She slid her arms around his neck.

"Will you accept me, Sarah?" he asked, his voice low with desire. "I need to hear you say it."

But she had forgotten how to speak, how to think. She slid her open palms down his chest, just like she had wanted to do before.

He sucked in a breath and held perfectly still, allowing her to mold her hands to his pecs, his ribs, his abs.

When she slid them down lower, he caught her wrists in his big hand.

"Enough," he growled.

But she could sense the aching throb of his desire, how badly he wanted her hands on him.

She moaned lightly and he leaned in to swallow the sound, pressing his lips to hers.

He tasted like sunlight.

She let him thumb her jaw open, let him consume her mouth as her body sang and pulsed.

When he pulled away, she nearly cried with unsatisfied need.

But he was only pulling back to coax her all the way into the soft bed, so that her head rested on the pillows, and then he lay beside her, fixing her in his topaz gaze.

"Zane," she managed to murmur.

"I know, my love," he whispered. "You want me so much it hurts. I want you too, little one, but not until you decide to accept me as your mate."

She moaned in frustration.

"Let me comfort you," he whispered, leaning down to press a kiss to her forehead.

His touch sent her into a haze again, she felt his warm lips caress her eyelids, her cheeks, her neck. Zane groaned as he nibbled the place where her neck met her shoulder and the sound reverberated through her, sending shivers down her spine.

He kissed his way down the low neck of her gown. She'd almost forgotten she was still wearing the frivolous garment the Agency had supplied.

There was a tearing sound, and when she looked down, she saw he had ripped it in half.

Good. I hate this gown. I want nothing between us.

But he was nuzzling her breasts and all thought left her mind as he licked one nipple into his mouth and rolled the other between his thumb and forefinger.

Sarah arched her back, longing for more.

Zane growled and fed on her breasts with abandon until she was crying out for more.

He rubbed his rough jaw against the tender skin of her

belly as he lowered himself downward, ripping her panties in half with another quick movement.

Sarah wavered between embarrassment and desire. No man had ever touched her there, but she was restless with desperate need.

When he nudged her legs, she let them fall apart for him, shameless in her need for his touch.

"Sarah," he murmured as he pressed kisses to her inner thighs.

She let her head fall back as she took in the sensation of his warm breath against her sex, and then his tongue...

The world seemed to disappear from around them. There were only the soft, gentle movements of his warm mouth, and the wild, frantic pulse at her core as he coaxed her higher and higher until her hips trembled. It was all she could do to stop herself from tangling her hands in his hair and grinding herself into that clever mouth.

"Please," she whimpered, helpless.

Instantly he increased the pressure of his mouth, flicking his tongue against her most sensitive spot as he eased a finger just inside her opening.

Sarah was soaring, the pleasure lifting her higher and higher, then pulsing down on her in waves of ecstasy that left her shivering and moaning.

12

ZANE

Zane crawled up beside Sarah and pulled her into his arms.

He was burning with need for her, his body racked with desire, his soul crying out to be joined with hers.

But he would not claim her until she begged.

Forever, he reminded himself.

He would not bind her to him forever if she had any doubts.

But her arms were going around his neck and she was pressing her bare body close, as if urging him to forget his determination to be patient.

"No, my love," he whispered to her. He could hear the naked desire in his own voice.

"Don't you... want me?" she asked him.

He pressed his lips to her forehead again.

"I want you so much," he assured her. "So much that it hurts, but we won't seal our bond until I know it's what you want."

She was quiet for a moment.

"Can I help you like you helped me?" she offered quietly.

He closed his eyes and counted to ten, trying desperately not to think of her sweet mouth on his rigid cock.

"No," he whispered through a taut jaw. "Let's get some rest. Bowen will wake us before dawn."

She snuggled into his chest and he stroked her back until her breathing slowed.

He lay awake for a long time, waiting for the pounding of his own pulse to slow.

He must have fallen asleep at some point, because he awoke with his arms around her. It was still dark, but he could hear Bowen making soft, wakeful sounds in his room down the hall.

He let Sarah go regretfully, sliding out of bed and replacing himself with a pillow and another blanket. Sarah snuggled in, her forehead slightly furrowed.

Good. She should feel incomplete without me.

But he bent to brush her hair with his lips. When he straightened, he could see she was smiling slightly in her sleep.

He headed out to the hallway and ducked into Bowen's room. The baby was kicking his little feet and smiling up at the mobile that floated over his crib. Tiny dragons - he wasn't sure whether to be flattered or offended.

"Good morning, whelp," he told the boy.

Bowen squeaked back and smiled, dimples on full display.

"Let's find some breakfast," Zane said, lifting the babe in his arms.

Bowen banged his head on Zane's chest in agreement and grabbed a hank of his hair for good measure.

"You're very hungry," Zane said, impressed. "You are growing."

Bowen made noises of spirited agreement, though Zane was sure the boy didn't understand what he had said. They headed into the main area of the house, and Zane checked out the contents of the kitchen.

It was fairly well stocked. There was no produce, so they would have to shop soon. But the ice box held plenty of milk, eggs, and butter, and there were dry and canned ingredients in the cupboard over the stove.

He warmed some milk and cereal for Bowen and thought over what he could cook while he fed the boy.

"I think Sarah will like hen's bread," he told Bowen. "What do you think?"

But Bowen was eating as fast as he could. He had no time for talking.

Zane put Bowen in a play seat near the table when he was finished with his meal. The boy bounced and played happily with the plastic beads on the wire framework of the seat.

Based on Zane's experience, this happiness wouldn't last long. Bowen liked being held. There was limited time for cooking.

He put on a kettle for tea. Then he grabbed a frying pan and began cracking eggs and dipping in slices of thick bread.

Soon the griddle was sizzling, and he was flipping warm hen's bread onto plates.

Bowen had stopped playing with the beads to cackle at him and Zane was being a little silly about his work to amuse the boy.

Suddenly, he sensed his mate was near.

He looked up to see that Sarah was standing in the doorway, a shy smile on her face.

"How long have you been standing there?" he asked.

"Long enough," she teased. "I didn't know they made my grandmother's favorite breakfast on Ignis-7."

"We call it hen's bread," he said. "Bread dipped in eggs and milk and fried?"

"Exactly," she confirmed. "My grandmother always called it panperdy, though I never asked why."

"Do you like it?" he asked.

"I love it," she told him. "She used to make it for us as a special treat."

"Good, I hope you're hungry," he told her.

"I could get used to this," she said, sitting down at the table beside Bowen's play seat.

Immediately, the boy put his arms up to her, lower lip trembling.

"You can't fool me," she said, laughing as she got him out. "I saw how much fun you were having."

"He really likes to be held," Zane explained.

"I really like holding him," Sarah said, kissing the boy on top of his fluffy head.

Zane felt a wave of love so intense he couldn't speak and had to turn back to the stove so Sarah wouldn't see the tears in his eyes.

He was an Invicta warrior. Warriors did not weep.

"So how long until dawn?" Sarah asked. "Do we have time to eat?"

"Of course," Zane told her. "Little Bowen knew just when to wake us."

He placed a plate of hen's bread in front of her and went back for his own, and the pot of tea.

"Thank you," Sarah said. "This is really nice - berries and everything."

"The berries came from a can," he warned her. "But I think it will be pretty good anyway."

He watched her take the first bite and then close her eyes in ecstasy.

Gods...

"Mmmm," she moaned over it.

"Good?" he managed to choke out.

"Unbelievable," she told him.

Bowen squawked at her, as if only just realizing that she had food and that maybe his breakfast had not been enough.

"Did you want some panperdy?" she asked him.

He whacked her chest with his chubby arm.

"Okay," she said, cutting off a tiny piece to feed to him.

He worked it in his mouth for a minute, eyes wide.

It was hard for Zane to tell whether the boy liked foods right away, this suspense while the whelp gave the bread a try was riveting.

"*Mah*," Bowen cried as soon as he had swallowed the bite.

"Oh, he likes it," Zane said.

There was quiet for a few minutes except for the clink of knives and forks and Bowen's imperious cries as they cut up tiny bites as fast as they could.

At last, Sarah held out a bite and Bowen let it fall out of his mouth.

"I think that means he's done," Zane laughed.

The boy yawned as if in agreement, and rested his head on Sarah's chest.

The scene was so peaceful. His mate and child enjoying a nice breakfast.

After the horrors he'd seen on the front lines of Falnnos, this felt almost like it couldn't be real.

"So, we're meeting Slade this morning," she said, breaking the spell.

He felt a wave of fury at the mention of the other man, though he had done nothing wrong.

"Can I ask you something?" she asked.

"Of course."

"Can't you just turn into a dragon and fly up to check out where Caldwell is?" she asked. "That isn't the same as taking him down. You would just be helping me find him."

"That's not the way this works, Sarah," he told her. "The Invicta can only shift to protect the mother land. And in my case, also to protect Bowen."

"So, last night...?" she began.

For a golden instant he thought she was going to bring up their mate bond. But then he remembered how he had shifted when the neighbors were there.

"That was to protect Bowen," he said. "I didn't know who was here."

Sarah looked disappointed, but she nodded.

It occurred to him that she was stubborn enough herself that she must respect that he had boundaries, too.

"Well, even if you won't help me, thank goodness Slade will," she said, standing and clearing their plates. "Are you ready?"

He nodded, too furious to reply.

Slade was only helping her for money. And because she was radiantly beautiful.

But there was nothing Zane could do about it. He would not defy the Invicta code just to make her like him.

She was going to have to like him for himself.

Deep in his chest the dragon roared and paced. He didn't care why Sarah liked him. He didn't care for any of this human nonsense.

His need to claim her was primal.

13

ZANE

Zane carried Bowen and kept an eye on Sarah as they walked through the blue-green meadow to the edge of town. She showed no signs of pain, at least not that he noticed. She wasn't even using the cane, although she still had it with her.

"What?" she asked him.

"I was just wondering if you were doing okay," he said. "Your leg?"

"I'm fine," she said, looking pleased. "I think it's the gravity. I'm half-tempted to take up gymnastics again."

"You were a gymnast?" he asked, fascinated.

"Not a real one," she laughed. "But I took classes when I was younger. It was fun."

"I can see you doing gymnastics," he decided.

"Well, maybe I will, once we get Caldwell squared away," she said.

He tried to picture what life would be like if she succeeded in taking out Jericho Caldwell, and suddenly the day didn't seem as beautiful.

"Oh my gosh, what's that?" Sarah asked breathlessly.

He glanced up to see what she had noticed.

Fucking Slade.

The young marshal had tacked up three beautiful stag-horses. He rode atop sleek black one with glistening antlers, and there was a long-maned, snowy one with bone-white antlers that must be for Sarah.

The third stag-horse was an enormous but scruffy looking gray-brown thing, with a sway back and a snarly tail.

"They're beautiful," Sarah called out to Slade, jogging ahead to get a better look at the animals.

"Show off," Zane muttered into Bowen's hair.

But Bowen didn't answer. The baby was snuggled in a sling around Zane's chest, where he had gone promptly to sleep as soon as they began walking.

Imberian babies slept *a lot.* In the beginning, Zane had thought something was wrong with the child.

While Bowen's generous sleep schedule often meant Zane could get things done, right now, he almost wished the boy would wake up and distract him from Sarah's ecstatic exclamations to Slade.

"Lachesis has many beautiful creatures," Slade was telling her. "We're bound to see some of the more terrifying ones today, too. But as long as you stay close, I'll see that no harm comes to you."

Zane imagined shifting into a dragon and roaring at Slade, just to watch him wet his pants.

Easy, boy, he reminded himself.

"Zane," Slade said, as if he were surprised. "Do you really think this is a good place for a baby?"

"I won't leave him with a stranger," Sarah said firmly, before Zane could even reply.

"As long as he stays close to me, no harm will come to

him," Zane said flatly, with maybe just a tiny hint of sarcasm.

But Slade either didn't recognize his own words coming back to him, or didn't care.

"I brought this big fellow for you," he said, shrugging and pointing to the big sway-backed beast. "The white one is yours, Miss Flynn."

"Call me Sarah," she said.

Slade tipped his hat to her in a very gratified way.

Zane was trying to decide whether to punch him in the nose when his stag-horse brayed at him. He turned to the beast and it gazed back at him, its chocolate brown eyes slightly widened.

"Smells the dragon on you," Slade suggested. "He'll gentle down soon enough."

Zane certainly hoped so. He didn't mind getting thrown himself, but he had the baby to think of.

"Easy, friend," he said to the stag-horse in a low, calm voice.

It shifted its weight on its slender legs and blinked at him. He lifted his hand slowly, and scratched gently at the base of the antlers. The creature closed its eyes and leaned into his touch.

Sarah laughed, and he looked up to see that Slade had helped her onto her mount.

It was a young, restless thing, and it pranced under her as if it wanted to run.

Zane bit back words of judgement.

But he couldn't help thinking them. Slade might not know about Sarah's leg. But he also didn't know if she could ride or not. He was clearly more worried about impressing her with a pretty steed than about keeping her safe.

To her credit, Sarah was sticking her seat nicely and

murmuring to the mare. It seemed likely that she was an experienced rider, if not of stag-horses, then of something similar from her homeworld.

"This is amazing," she called to Zane with a radiant smile.

He smiled back at her and waved.

"Let's go, dragon," Slade yelled to him, remounting his onyx stallion, which immediately pranced up beside Sarah's mare.

"Let's get this over with," Zane whispered to Bowen.

14

SARAH

The morning stretched out for Sarah in a sort of endless joyride.

Her stag-mare was nimble and light-footed. Though she had been a little skittish at first, she had gentled right away under Sarah's touch. Now, the pretty creature seemed to take pleasure in flying across the shadowy meadows, her mane and tail flowing out behind her in the low gravity, like a storybook pony.

They moved as one, the mare's smooth gait making the long ride seem effortless, leaving Sarah to enjoy the fragrance of the trees and flowers, and the way the dappled light painted the approaching hillside.

The only thing troubling her was Zane. The big alien didn't seem to be enjoying the trip or the scenery. He rode with a serious expression, eyes narrowed.

Slade, on the other hand, seemed to be reveling in their excursion.

"We're making excellent time," he called to Sarah as he brought his inky stallion up to join her. "But we should slow down now. We're getting close."

"How do you know?" Sarah asked, pulling up her mare to a trot to cool her down.

"I did a little research around town last night," Slade said, tipping his wide-brimmed hat and looking rather pleased with himself. "It seems our bounty has been spending time with Dirty Al and Billaxx, two local petty criminals. They sometimes camp out on the other side of that rise."

"So, what's the plan?" Sarah asked.

"We go up to the bluff and see if we can catch sight of them below," Slade said. "Without them catching sight of us, that is."

She glanced back at Zane.

He nodded once, as if to bless the plan.

They all rode on in silence, the stag-horses picking their way up the hill as the sun began to set.

An hour later, they had all dismounted at the peak of the low bluff.

Sarah held Bowen and fed him a snack as Slade belly crawled out on the ledge to look down on the valley below. It wasn't far down, but they had a pretty good vantage point.

"He's hungry," Zane said, gazing at the baby as he ate.

"He had a long day," Sarah said, smiling at her little one.

He was eating his mush as fast as she could spoon it into his mouth.

"Was he awake for much of the ride?" she asked Zane.

"I thought he would sleep the whole time," Zane said. "But he woke up as soon as we started really moving. He seemed to like watching the world fly past. He'll sleep well tonight."

Sarah nodded, hoping Bowen would sleep while they were in pursuit. She didn't like the idea of him making a noise that would give them away.

And she really didn't like the idea of him being in danger. As little as she wanted to leave him behind, she was suddenly having second thoughts about having him here.

"I will not allow one hair on his head to come to harm," Zane said softly, as if he had read her mind.

She lifted her chin to look into his eyes.

This man, this dragon, wanted to be her mate - to be with her forever, to care for her and protect her with the same devotion he showed to Bowen.

The idea felt real to her now, anchoring her in this feather-light place, lighting the murky-darkness.

"Zane," she murmured, lost in the intensity of his azure gaze.

"Okey-dokey," Slade said, brushing leaves off his breeches as he approached. "They're down there, all right, but Caldwell's not with them, at least not yet. We should keep an eye on them."

Sarah tried to focus on what he was saying. But it didn't seem to make sense.

"You mean just... wait?" Sarah asked.

"Not much else we can do," Slade said.

"We can question them," she said. "We can march right down there and question them."

"If he comes back, then we'll know where he is for sure," Slade pointed out. "If we question them, they may not answer."

"Then you'll make them answer," Sarah said. "Are you a trained marshal or not?"

"I am, but this isn't the way it's normally done," Slade spluttered.

"Why not give it a little time?" Zane asked, surprising her by taking Slade's side.

"Because it's going to get dark, and they're going to slip away," she said. "If you're not going down there, I am."

"Okay," Zane said, raising his hands up. "Let me put Bowen on your back so you can run if you have to. You'll stay up here and keep watch, and we'll go down there and check things out."

"You can put him on my back. That's a good idea," Sarah said, carefully leaving out the part where he was crazy if he thought she was staying behind.

She waited while he loaded up the baby. When Bowen's warm weight was snuggly wrapped on her back, and his chubby fists tangled in her hair, she turned back to the others.

"What are they doing down there?" she asked Slade.

"They're getting a campfire going," he said.

"So the light from the fire will make it easier to sneak up on them," she replied.

"True," Zane said, eyeing her thoughtfully.

"Do you have weapons?" she asked Slade.

He grinned and pulled a shiny, silver long-pistol from his coat. It gleamed in the fading light, showing off intricate engravings.

"She's a beaut, isn't she?" he asked Zane. "What are you packing?"

"No guns needed," Zane said gruffly.

"Oh right," Slade said. "You'll be in dragon form?"

He sounded almost disappointed.

"No, man, it's not a parlor trick," Zane said. "I can fight just fine with my hands if I have to."

"Suit yourself," Slade said with a shrug.

"You'll stay here with the stag-horses?" Zane asked Sarah.

"I won't," she said. "But they're tied up, so I'm sure they'll be fine."

"You can't come down there unarmed," Zane said sharply.

"I'm not unarmed," she told him, sliding her cane apart to reveal the slender, silver sword hidden within. She'd been afraid they wouldn't let her bring it to Lachesis, but no one had even asked about it.

"Nice," Slade said appreciatively.

"I don't want you down there," Zane said.

"Then it's a good thing you're not in charge of me," she replied.

"I'm in charge of that whelp on your back," he retorted.

"You're in charge of *protecting* him," she said. "I'm his mother. But if you're worried about it, you can just shift and take care of this all by yourself."

He opened his mouth and closed it again.

"That's what I thought," she said. "Let's go."

She knew she should wait for the others, but she was tired of waiting.

Sarah Flynn was ready for justice.

15

SARAH

Though Sarah marched off briskly, Slade and Zane overtook her swiftly.

As a matter of fact, they seemed to be in a walking race.

She watched them in wonder. Men were mysterious creatures.

Sarah had done her fair share of dating, even had a guy or two she was somewhat serious with, but it hadn't worked out for one reason or another.

Her father was the only man she had ever felt she really understood. He was different from the blustery roosters like these two.

Reginald Bowen Flynn was calm and gentle. He never did anything without a reason.

Sarah remembered following him around, asking endless questions as a child, and each action he took had a careful explanation - from the biggest things right down to whether he put the peanut butter on her muffin first or the jam. He was a deliberate person.

The men in front of her right now, on the other hand...

Sarah doubted they could tell her why they were behaving so strangely even if she asked. There seemed to be an unconscious competitive streak in men that caused them to do inexplicable things.

They reached the edge of the bluff and began slowly picking their way down.

When she caught up at the bottom of the bluff, she could see the villains silhouetted in the glow of the campfire just ahead.

By some miracle, Dirty Al and Billaxx had their backs to the bluff and were looking out over the plane.

She knew immediately which one was Dirty Al, his greasy yellow hair hung down his back under a gray hat that she strongly suspected used to be white. He stood by the fire, placing a pan on a rock at its center. A scraggly-looking mule of some sort grazed on the short grass behind them.

The one called Billaxx was a Maltaffian, with massive horns on his head. He was leaned back, watching Dirty Al dump a can of beans into a pan over the flames.

Ahead of her, Slade was crouched low, his pistol raised and gleaming in the firelight as he moved forward.

Zane had stopped and was waiting for her, a pleading look in his blue eyes.

He wanted her to wait.

She could feel his fear through the bond. It was fear for her, but for Bowen as well.

A pang of guilt went through her chest. If anything happened to the baby, she would never forgive herself.

Suddenly, she thought of her father and the way he reasoned everything he did. But this time, she thought of him in light of her own actions.

Was it better for her to follow Zane and Slade than to hang back with Bowen?

No.

She nodded to Zane, letting him know she would wait.

The relief in his eyes was palpable.

She almost felt guilty, but then she remembered that if he was so worried, he could have just taken his dragon form and handled this problem all by himself.

The Invicta might have rules, but the Invicta weren't here. If Zane was committed to twenty years with Bowen, and forever with Sarah, he might have to think about his priorities. Things were different on the frontier.

But before she could continue down that train of thought, Slade reached the men at the fire.

In a flash, he had his gun pointed at Billaxx's horned head.

"Okay, scumbags," Slade shouted. "I'm only going to ask this once. Where's Caldwell?"

"I don't know who you mean," the Maltaffian growled.

"Oh no?" Slade asked.

There was a loud click as he thumbed back the hammer on his gun.

Zane moved around the fire toward Dirty Al, neatly stepping around a pile of dinged-up china plates that must have been waiting for their dinner.

But before Zane could reach him, Dirty Al swung around and kicked a log from the fire in Zane's direction.

The dragon warrior easily dodged the log, but a cloud of ash and sparks tumbled through the air, right into Zane's face.

Slade coughed and spluttered.

In the seconds it bought them, Billaxx and Dirty Al ran in opposite directions.

"They're getting away," Sarah pleaded.

Zane wiped his eyes with an arm and took off in the direction of Billaxx.

Slade blinked and brushed the dust off his suit before following Dirty Al toward the meadow.

Sarah thought for a moment and headed out after Zane and Billaxx. Something told her the Maltaffian was the smarter and better informed of the two ruffians.

And something inside her pulled taut with every step that Zane took away from her.

The low gravity made running a pleasure, there was no pain, even with Bowen on her back. But she was nowhere near as fast as the two large men.

She focused on keeping them in sight. If she could just keep her eyes on Zane, everything would be okay.

She was sure of it.

16

ZANE

Zane ran as fast as he could, still blinking the grit out of his eyes.

It was lucky he had been the closer one to the fire. The sparks hadn't burned his eyes the way they would have burned Slade's. His dragon's abilities were part of his skill set, whether he was using them consciously or not. And dragons didn't burn.

He wondered what his commander would think of him, taking on a mission that had nothing to do with his homeland. He wasn't shifting, but was that really enough to make this behavior acceptable?

There was no time to think about it. He had committed to a course of action, and now the only thing he could do was try to help Sarah without allowing any harm to come to her.

At least he was gaining on Billaxx, and that was a relief.

On and on they ran, through a field of purple dawn flowers and over the rocky terrain of what seemed to be a dry riverbed. With grit still in his eyes, it was hard for Zane to see exactly, but there was no time to stop and clean them out while he was close enough to hear the Maltaffian panting.

He had nearly caught up to his quarry, when Billaxx hung a sharp left around an outcropping of stones and Zane followed.

He reached out an arm as he rounded the corner, hoping to catch hold of Billaxx's shoulder.

But the Maltaffian ducked at the last moment.

Zane didn't see the tree branch at eye level until it was too late. He hit it hard enough to crack the branch in half and whip his own head backward, landing on his posterior on the rocky ground.

He could hear the Maltaffian cackling as he took off and fury rose in his throat.

He closed his eyes for a moment, allowing his shifter abilities to heal his eyes, his head, his neck, and his bruised butt.

Then he leaped up and tore after his opponent with fresh energy.

Billaxx had made a fatal error. He had assumed Zane would be down for more than a second. He was jogging now, trying to catch his breath.

By the time he heard Zane's footsteps behind him and turned, it was too late.

Zane collared him easily and wrapped the villain's hands behind his back in a leather thong, faster than the Maltaffian could follow what was happening.

"Seriously?" Billaxx complained.

"You may be just a petty criminal yourself, but you're aiding and abetting a known felon," Zane said. "Now, either walk with me, or I'll throw you over my shoulder like the sack of potatoes you have the sense of, whichever you prefer."

Billaxx scoffed, but he walked along agreeably enough.

Zane chose to stay silent and let the guy worry about what was going to happen next.

By the time they reached the foot of the bluff again, the Maltaffian was decidedly subdued. Zane hoped it might help them get the info they needed.

Unfortunately, Slade was already standing there, practically tapping his foot.

Dirty Al was tied up next to the fire.

It figured that the scrawny Terran had been easier to catch.

"Kind of you to join us," Slade teased.

Zane narrowed his eyes, but didn't reply. Slade had just broken the first rule of encounters with the captured. Allies had to have each other's backs. There could be no chink in the armor - no matter how small.

"Are you all ready to talk?" Slade asked.

But their prisoners didn't reply.

Slade reached into a pouch on his belt and pulled out an ancient-looking comms tablet. He swiped at it a few times and a familiar image appeared on the screen.

"I see there's a warrant out for the arrest of a Maltaffian who goes by the moniker of Billaxx," Slade went on. "I could bring you in for this vandalism charge. Or for the drunk and disorderly from last Moon Fest."

Slade began to pace, looking up at the stars and then subconsciously rubbing his marshal's badge as he spoke.

"But it could turn out that you gave us the slip tonight," he said. "If you were willing to tell us where Caldwell is. You boys might not be aware, but he's a bad man. He killed the father of that little lady over there."

Slade pointed to Sarah, who was watching everything, wide-eyed, from the shadows at the foot of the bluff.

Zane swallowed down a bellow of rage.

Why would Slade draw their attention to his mate? There was no reason for them to even realize she was there.

Slade was a thoughtless diva, more concerned with his pride filled monologue than with actually solving their problem.

"We, uh, didn't realize he was in that kind of trouble," Billaxx said.

"Changes your mind about where your loyalties, lie, eh?" Slade asked knowingly, pacing over to Billaxx. "So, tell us, big guy, where is he?"

Billaxx paused.

Slade kicked him gently with the tip of his fancy leather boot. "Talk or don't talk. We don't have all night."

"The old riverbed," Billaxx said quickly. "If you follow it north, it leads to a cave. He's camping out in there."

"A cave?" Slade echoed.

"Yeah," Billaxx said. "You might want to approach real slow. He's pretty skittish."

"Appreciate your help, son," Slade said, igniting a small energy-blade he pulled from his pocket, and releasing the Maltaffian from his bonds. "Don't get yourself into any more trouble. Steer clear of Jericho Caldwell. Do you hear me?"

"Yeah, we gotcha," Billaxx said, stretching out his arms.

Slade released Dirty Al as well, and watched them gather their things and pack them onto the scrawny beggars-mule. Before they moved on, Dirty Al pulled a few handfuls of the purple flowers from the side of the path and dumped them on the fire, smothering it in a big puff of fragrant smoke. Once it was out, the two men went on their way.

"Why are you standing there?" Sarah asked, stalking up

once the men had disappeared from view. "Let's get the horses and head down that riverbed."

"We're not going down that riverbed," Slade said, still watching after the two criminals.

"What are you talking about?" Sarah demanded. "We had a deal. You were going to help us find him."

"And I intend to, ma'am," Slade said, turning to her with an infuriating flourish. "But that's not where he is."

"What are you talking about?" Sarah said. "We just heard them. You threatened them, and they told you."

"Did you notice the flatware?" Slade asked her, his eyes twinkling.

"Sure," she said,

Zane thought back to the chipped plates and cups on the grass when he'd first approached the fire.

"How many did you see?" Slade asked.

"Three," Sarah said softly.

"Three," Slade said, nodding and practically patting himself on the back. "Which means they were expecting company. Now the first thing those two knuckleheads will do is run and warn Caldwell. All we need to do is follow. They're going to lead us right to him."

Damnit. The cocky bastard was right.

Zane glowered at him, as Sarah's eyes lit up in admiration.

17
____

SARAH

Sarah smiled at Slade. She was half-tempted to applaud.

Though there had been moments throughout the day when she had wondered if hiring him would pay off, he had just proven himself worth his weight in electrum rods.

"Very nice," she said. "But he can't be far off if he was planning to join them for dinner. We'd better not let them out of our sight."

"That smoke signal they sent up on the way out of here will have warned him off," Slade explained. "He'll know not to come here. Most likely, they have a regular meeting place."

"So, what do we do?" Sarah asked.

"If they see us, they'll lead us on a wild goose chase," Slade said. "We'll follow, but slowly."

"What if we lose them?" she asked.

"Look at those jokers," he said with a smile. "They're going to leave a trail a mile wide. I could follow it in my sleep."

Sarah glanced over at Zane, uncertain.

"Look, ma'am, you hired the best tracker on Lachesis for a reason," Slade said. "Let me track."

Zane rolled his eyes.

Sarah giggled before she could stop herself, but managed to turn it into what she hoped was a convincing cough.

"Thank you, Slade," she said, turning back to him. "I'll follow your counsel."

"Good," he said, tipping his hat to her. "Let's go back to our mounts. We'll follow along enough to get a sense of which way they're headed. Then we'll need to find a place to get some sleep, some place out of sight."

Sarah nearly screamed at the idea that they would have to stop overnight. They were so close...

"Sounds good," Zane said, his deep voice awakening something in Sarah's heart. "They'll have to rest, too."

They headed back up the bluff, picking their way over rocks and roots. Coming down had been easier. But she'd also had adrenaline on her side. By the time they reached the peak, she was glad they were planning to get some rest.

Her stag-mare whickered at the sight of her, and Sarah stroked the mare's silky cheek, wishing she had a treat to give her.

"When we get settled, we can feed them too," Slade said softly.

Sarah nodded and loosened the mare's reins from the tree where she had secured them.

"Are you okay to keep carrying Bowen?" Zane asked as she prepared to mount.

"I'm fine," she told him. "Does he look happy?"

"He's awake," Zane said. "And he seems content. Hopefully, he won't get hungry again until we get wherever we're going."

"Hopefully," Sarah said, suddenly wondering what she was supposed to do if he started fussing while he was on her back.

"He likes going for a ride," Zane reassured her. "He'll be just fine. Want a hand up?"

She let him help her onto the mare, though she didn't really need help.

His big hands felt good on her body and she couldn't help but remember what happened between them last night.

I am your mate.

It felt surreal to think that less than a day had passed since they had shared her bed. And now they were out on the plains, chasing down Jericho Caldwell, with a marshal in tow.

"Ready?" Slade called to them, one eyebrow arched.

"Yes," she said quickly as Zane let her go and headed to his own mount.

"Look up there," Slade told her, bringing his stallion up to her mare and pointing at a ridge across the plain. "There should be caves in that rocky area."

"Of course," she said crisply, though the idea of sleeping in a cave was horrifying. She was a city girl after all.

Justice delayed is justice denied.

The quote got her head in the game again, and she squeezed the mare's belly gently with her ankles to urge her to follow Slade's stallion.

The mare ambled down the incline and Sarah was struck all over again at the impact of the lowered gravity. Her leg should have been jostled and banged up mercilessly, leaving her moaning in pain.

Instead, it felt like she was a rag doll, or the air was really water. She smiled at the thought that she could live a normal life on this moon when the hunt for Caldwell was over.

As normal a life as she could if she had killed a man.

She tried not to think about what might happen to her if the police force of Lachesis decided to hold her accountable for what she was about to do.

On the one hand, hiring a marshal to help her meant she was going to find Caldwell.

On the other, it meant she would have a police witness when she killed him.

Maybe she should have told Slade that part of his pay was to keep his mouth shut when it was all over. But then he might not have agreed to help at all.

The most important thing she could do right now was to keep her eye on the prize. She had come all this way to ensure that Caldwell could never kill again, never ruin another family's life. She couldn't let herself get caught up in what happened to her. She would go to jail a thousand times to put her own family back together again. Doing it once to save someone else's seemed a small price to pay.

They reached the meadow, and the stag-horses began to let loose.

She intentionally released her mind from everything but the feel of the wind lifting her hair as the horses streaked across the moonlit meadow toward the ridge.

18

———

SARAH

Sarah looked around the stone face of the ridge.

They had found a place to tie up their mounts out of sight almost immediately. A natural spring let out a continuous trickle of sweet water against the rock face that the horses were lapping at eagerly while she and Zane emptied their grain onto the ground at their feet. It wasn't fancy but the stag-horses seemed delighted.

Slade had gone poking around the rocks to see if he could find a big enough cave for them to sleep in.

Sarah half hoped he wouldn't find anything. A little claustrophobia coupled with a dislike for creepy crawly things made a cave sound like a bad place to sleep. And the more she thought about it, the more she didn't like the whole idea.

But there was no point worrying about it. Slade had done this before. She was sure he wouldn't lead them astray.

"A credit for your thoughts," Zane said softly.

"I'm just fretting about sleeping in a cave," she laughed.

"So, chasing down a hardened criminal is fine with you, but you're afraid of spiders?" Zane teased.

"Not really," she told him. "I just got spoiled by having a house of my own."

He turned to her, his eyes twinkling. "We'll be home again soon enough."

Home again...

But Sarah might never go home again, not after what she was about to do.

"Hey, I found the perfect cave," Slade said as he came around the corner, holding a chem-lantern. "Are the mounts settled in?"

"Sure are," Sarah said quickly. "Let's see this cave."

They followed him around to a dark opening in the rock face.

Sarah hung back slightly, unable to make herself move forward.

"Here," Slade said, holding up the lantern and moving inside.

The circle of light filled the space. The rock floor of the cave was surprisingly smooth, but the walls were pocked with fist-sized, dark holes.

"Don't worry," Slade said. "Those are just prairie mouse holes."

Sarah shuddered at the thought of wild mice big enough to need those holes, but Zane put his hand at the small of her back.

"They're harmless," he whispered into her hair.

A shiver went down her back and she found she didn't care so much about prairie mice anymore.

Slade set the lantern at the center of the cave and they began to lay out their things. Once the floor was covered in bed rolls, Zane lifted Bowen off of Sarah's back. The little one prattled happily, smacking Zane's cheeks with his little hands, the sounds of his happiness echoing off the cave walls.

Zane sat him on a bed roll, where he looked around with wide eyes.

Sarah began buttering a few of the slabs of bread she had packed with them.

"We'll take turns keeping watch," Slade said, pouring out a mug of cold water from his thermoflask. "But I think we'll have a quiet night."

Bowen squeaked, and Sarah looked over to see that bright blue cricket sitting on the bed roll beside him.

"Harmless," Slade assured her. "Azure cave crickets are very common on Lachesis. They're a good source of protein too, if you ever get desperate out here. With a little seasoning, they're not half bad."

Sarah wrinkled her nose and kept buttering bread.

Bowen cooed at the cricket and then clapped his little hands together as a second and third came to join the first.

"Cheerful little fella," Slade said appreciatively. "I had a bunch of little brothers. Kids are fun to have around."

Sarah smiled fondly at Bowen. He *was* fun to have around.

Another cave cricket hopped onto the blanket.

Faster than she could track it, something flew out of a hole in the wall and snapped up one of the bugs.

Bowen squealed with delight as he watched the thing stop to chew.

Sarah's heart went cold as ice.

It was a snake-like creature, massive, with yellow-slitted eyes and striped markings. About a meter of it was protruding from the wall, but that huge, ribbony body could go on forever inside the rock for all she knew.

Zane began to move toward Bowen.

"Freeze," Slade snapped, stopping Zane in his tracks. "They're attracted to movement."

"Wh-what is that?" Sarah murmured, her eyes fixed on her son, who was chattering away happily at the horrifying thing.

"That's a cave eel," Slade said. "They have a venomous bite, and even the slime on their skin is toxic. You don't want to touch it."

Sarah felt her knees go weak and the blood rush away from her head, but she forced herself to remain alert, eyes on Bowen.

"Everything will be fine, as long as we're nice and slow, and no one makes any sudden movements," Slade murmured as he stretched out slowly for the strap of his gun, which was leaned against the cave wall just out of his reach.

Sarah watched as his fingers grazed the leather strap.

But instead of dropping into his hand, the gun fell to the cave floor with a clatter.

After that, everything seemed to happen in slow motion.

The eel drew back to strike, its yellow eyes flashing with fury.

Quicker than she thought possible, Zane threw himself to the ground in front of Bowen, wrapping the baby in his arms and rolling to the side.

The eel struck, hitting Zane in the leg.

Zane's roar of pain was echoed by the sound of a gunshot.

Sarah turned to see Slade, holding his gun, smoke issuing from the long barrel.

There was a thud as the eel hit the cave floor before it could strike again.

19

SARAH

"Zane," Sarah screamed, crawling over to him.

"He'll be fine," Slade said. "He's a dragon, remember? He's venomous himself."

She hadn't considered that, and didn't have any idea if it was true. But Slade sounded pretty certain. Of course, he'd also been pretty certain they'd find nothing but harmless prairie mice in those holes.

She moved to Zane, who was still curled protectively around Bowen. She rolled him onto his back and pulled the baby out of his arms.

"*Mah*," Bowen cried imperiously, smacking her on top of her head.

"Hi, baby," she murmured, kissing an impossibly soft golden cheek as she gazed down at his protector.

Zane was alive, but knocked out. He looked peaceful.

She reached out slowly and touched his jaw as Slade crawled up behind her.

"Hey," Zane said, his blue eyes blinking open suddenly and then narrowing at Slade. "Don't you look at my woman."

His words were slurred, as if he'd been drinking.

"What's wrong with him?" Sarah asked.

"It's the venom," Slade said in an embarrassed tone. "It's making him act a little silly. It will wear off."

"I said, *don't look at my woman*," Zane said. "You cocky country bumpkin."

"I'm not your woman," Sarah told him firmly, before Slade could take offense. "Now you rest until you've sobered up."

"*You*," Zane said, resting his eyes on Sarah. "Mate bond. Best thing ever happen to me," he declared. "If I can stop ya' from wreckin' it."

She blinked at him, willing him not to tell Slade her plans. If the marshal knew she was only looking for Caldwell so she could kill him, he might just leave them on their own.

It must have worked. Instead of revealing her vengeance scheme, he broke into song.

"*Beautiful as Lumen's pond,*
Took my love and sealed the bond,
Kisses sweet as wild honey,
Lick my lover on the—"

"Enough," Sarah yelped. "There is no need to sing your bawdy songs in front of the baby."

"Baby," Zane cooed. "Baby boy. There he is."

Bowen was too busy eating the bread Sarah still had clutched in her hand to take any notice of him. Zane sang in a soothing, lullaby way to the baby.

There was a pretty lassie picking flowers in the dell,
A laddie came one afternoon, before her heart he fell,
He gave her his love letters and a comb of tortoise shell,

But he never made the lass that picks her flowers in the dell.

IT STILL SOUNDED like the beginning of a bawdy song to Sarah, but Bowen had dropped the bread and was crawling toward Zane's arms as he sang on.

THERE WAS *a pretty lassie picking flowers in the dell,*
A gentleman was passing and before her heart he fell,
He gave her bands of burnished gold to ring the wedding bell,
But he never made the lass that picks her flowers in the dell.

BOWEN SNUGGLED into his chest and went promptly to sleep.

THERE WAS *a pretty lassie picking flowers in the dell,*
A dragon came to court her, and before her heart he fell,
He gave her his protection and she fell under his spell,
And the dragon made the lassie...

ZANE'S SONG trailed off into a loud snore.

"He's a loyal friend," Slade said, a smile in his voice.

"With a loud voice," Sarah agreed.

"Listen, I'll take the first watch," Slade said. "Unless you'd like me to stay with you a while longer?"

There was a hopeful glow in his hazel eyes, and she remembered that she had first thought the marshal was handsome.

But the drunk and sleeping dragon had a hold on her heart.

"I'm fine," she told him. "But bring some supper up there with you."

"Mighty obliged," he said, watching her pack up a mug of soup and a few wedges of buttered bread.

"Do I need to worry about more eels?" Sarah asked.

"No, ma'am," he replied. "I'll dispose of this one. They're rare, and extremely territorial. There won't be another one for miles."

"Good," she said, nodding, and hoping she could believe him. "Then I guess I'll try to get some sleep myself."

20

ZANE

Zane awoke in the darkness of a strange, cold place.

His dragon senses kicked in to tell him that the figure moving in the shadows nearby was his mate.

"Sarah?" he murmured.

His voice was strange and raspy, as if he had been screaming.

No.

He had been singing.

The events of the night before crowded back into his mind all at once and he sat up, clutching his head in his hands.

Bowen was sleeping beside him, his little hands splayed out like starfish.

And Sarah was sitting on the edge of the bedroll, lacing up her boots.

"Where are you going?" he asked her.

"Someone has to relieve the marshal," she said. "And you're in no condition to do it."

"I'm fine now. But Sarah..." He trailed off, uncertain how to even address last night.

"About that stuff you said," she murmured, turning to him.

"What stuff?" he asked. If he was remembering correctly, he had said a *lot* of stuff.

"About the mate bond," she said. "About it being the best thing that ever happened to you?"

"I meant it," he told her. "I know I said it like a buffoon, and I seem to remember following it up with some, er, singing."

"Yes, *several* songs were sung." She was trying not to smile, but he could see her eyes twinkling.

Thank the gods she has a sense of humor.

"You and Bowen give me purpose," he told her gruffly. "I don't want you to rush into any decisions. But I hope you'll accept my claim, Sarah Flynn."

She nodded while looking down at her hands, and he wondered what she was thinking.

He could sense sadness through their tenuous bond, which was unexpected when he was declaring his feelings.

"I'm a soldier, Sarah," he told her. "Not a poet. I wish I had the words to tell you better how you make me feel."

"Maybe a little more eel venom would help you express yourself?" she asked and then quirked an eyebrow at him.

He found himself laughing, the sound echoing off the walls around them.

Sarah laughed too, letting her head fall back slightly so that he could see the delicate column of her neck.

He pictured himself pressing his lips to her tender flesh, pinning her to the floor of this cave and staking his claim.

"Somebody woke up." Slade's annoying voice filled the cave.

"Yes, we're going to take the next shift," Zane said.

"Fantastic," Slade told him. "Are you feeling okay?"

"Never better," Zane said.

"I'll keep an eye on the little feller," Slade said, gazing down fondly at Bowen. "I had a baby brother. I know what to do if he wakes up."

"You'll come get me, that's what you'll do," Sarah told him firmly.

"Yes, ma'am," Slade assured her. "I can do that."

Sarah fixed him in her steely gaze for a moment. Whatever she saw must have satisfied her, because she nodded once and headed out of the cave.

Zane scrambled after her, nearly smashing his head on the rocky ceiling.

The air outside was cool and fresh. A light breeze rustled the long grasses in the meadow below and lifted Sarah's dark hair as he followed her to the top of the rocky ledge.

She lowered herself to the ground and sat with her legs curled under her. He sat beside her, and they gazed out over the starlit fields together for a long moment without saying anything.

"What are we looking out for, exactly?" Sarah asked after some time.

"Predators," Zane told her. "Big cats, and some canids live on the plains."

"Canids?" Sarah echoed.

"Blue wolves, wild dog-lets, that kind of thing," he explained. "Mostly they're just hungry. But they can be aggressive if they think you're trying to corner them."

Sarah nodded, looking nervous.

"The main thing to look out for is other sentient beings, though," he said. "People are far more dangerous to us than the natural wildlife here."

"Did you forget the eel?" Sarah asked.

"The eel just wanted something to eat," Zane said. "And

maybe some peace and quiet. He wasn't there specifically to hurt us."

"I guess you're right," she said, shaking her head. "But an animal can't be reasoned with."

"I know people who can't be reasoned with too," he said.

The moment the words were out of his mouth he wished he could take them back. She would think he was talking about her, and her mission of revenge. And if he was being honest, she wouldn't be totally wrong.

But she only nodded and looked down at her hands.

"Some things are beyond reason," she said softly.

He felt a wave of love and sadness in his chest. She was right. Her pain at the loss of her father was akin to the wild desire the bond inspired in him. There was no sense in even trying to argue with it.

"We don't ask for our feelings," he told her carefully. "And we can't control them."

She nodded.

"But we can try to channel them," he suggested. "Respond to them in ways that help us."

"I know what you're trying to do," she told him. "It won't work."

"Sarah, your father lost his life," he said, his resolve breaking. "Why should you lose yours trying to make it right?"

"I have to do this," she said.

"You can't bring him back," he told her, hating himself for his harshness.

"Oh," she said in a surprised way.

He looked up to see that a school of shiver birds was diving toward them in perfect formation, their silvery feathers shimmering like falling stars.

"What are they?" Sarah breathed.

For a moment, her expression of wonder reminded him of when Bowen had seen a school of the same little birds, right before they met her.

"Shiver birds," he told her. "They're harmless."

"They're almost like fish," she said as the school flew past, the air they displaced lifting her hair from her shoulders once more.

He reached out to touch the silky strands.

21

SARAH

Sarah held herself perfectly still as Zane ran his fingers through her hair.

He had done such things to her in bed, touching her in ways that made her toes curl.

But something about this was so much more intimate.

She could feel the bond between them. It was a delicate thing, but his touch played on it, like smoke revealing the beam of an infrared laser.

His eyes were so blue, and so sad.

She wished it wasn't so, but they were at an impasse. He was right to be sad.

An ocean of pleasure and happiness opened up before her, a future in which they would come to know and love each other, raise little Bowen, and tame a beautiful new moon.

But this was a sea she would not navigate.

"Zane, I can't," she whispered.

"I know," he told her, pulling her into his chest and cradling her there.

He was so warm. The comforting thump of his heart soothed her, and she let herself relax against him just for a moment.

She awoke sometime later to Bowen's crying.

"I think he wants you," Slade said awkwardly as he made his way up from the cave entrance with the grumpy baby in his arms.

She scrambled up, wondering how long she had been sleeping slumped against Zane's chest. Dawn light was already filtering through the cloud cover, giving the meadows that dappled, underwater look again.

She put her arms out for Bowen.

He reached for her right away, wriggling his way into her arms, making her heart sing, even though he was still wearing a grumpy expression, lower lip pouting and tears clinging to his eyelashes.

"We should get on the trail soon," Slade said. "I'll tend to the mounts."

"I'll just feed him, and we'll meet you down there," Sarah said.

Slade touched his cap and headed back down.

She turned back to Zane, but he was already standing and brushing off his breeches.

The intimate moment that had passed between them last night was gone now. In the dim light of dawn, she knew what she had to do, and she was pretty sure he wouldn't try to stop her.

"Big day ahead of us," she said.

Bowen squeaked at her and banged his head on her shoulder.

"Are you hungry, boy?" Zane asked him.

Bowen yelled and put his hands out for his protector.

Sarah let Zane take the little one, though her arms felt empty the moment he was gone.

Eyes on the prize, Sarah girl, she reminded herself.

But as they picked their way back down to the cave to prepare for the day, a pit of dread began to form in her belly.

22

ZANE

Zane was annoyed to find that once they were in the fields, the dapper marshal sniffed out the criminals' trail almost instantly, just as he had promised.

Realistically, he knew some of his dislike for the other man was jealousy over Sarah. But it was also hard not to resent his good humor.

"You see?" he was saying, holding up a bit of dirty paper. "This is the same cigarillo wrap the perps use in the holding cells on Hesiod-8. It's a dead giveaway."

"Wow," Sarah said, nodding.

"It would have been easy for them to clean up after themselves," Slade said in a pleased way.

"No one likes a litterbug," Sarah said.

"But they're certainly making my job simpler," Slade chuckled as he mounted his stallion.

Zane resisted the impulse to roll his eyes. He would have been able to do this tracking in his sleep using nothing more than his dragon's senses. But Sarah might as well get her money's worth out of this overstuffed rooster.

At least it would keep Slade occupied, so Zane would have more time to spend with Sarah.

He tried not to let himself hope he could change her mind.

"It's incredible out here," Sarah said, angling her mare up to join his horse.

He looked out over the blue-green meadow. The grasses waved rhythmically back and forth in the gentle breeze like seaweed in a gentle tide.

"It smells like the orchard my father took me to once on Terra-7," Sarah said dreamily.

"I thought you were a city girl," Zane said.

"Oh, I was," she told him. "This was a really special trip. We spent a month at an orchard after my dad had an especially successful tax season."

"Why an orchard?" Zane asked. "Don't most Terrans like beaches?"

"My father grew up on a farm," Sarah said. "He always wanted me to be more connected to nature."

Bowen squeaked at a massive butterfly that floated past.

It took no notice of him, but Sarah smiled fondly at the babe, and Zane felt his heart clench.

"Anyway, there was a huge harvest festival that year," she went on. "It was incredible to see all the fruits and vegetables and pies and cookies laid out on tables in the field by the little town hall. The air was so fresh you could taste it, just like this."

"So, you liked the countryside?" Zane asked.

"Until the last week," she said, frowning. "We were renting rooms at a farmhouse and they had a hutch full of rabbits. The farmer's daughter, Crayf, was about my age. She would play with them, and I did too. They were such pretty things, with long floppy ears and fur so soft it was like touching the breeze."

"Rabbits are the ones that jump, right?" Zane asked.

"Yes, exactly," she agreed. "Anyway, her father had been having problems with a fox that kept getting into their hen house. The farmer wanted to shoot him, but Crayf begged him not to. She was tenderhearted, and didn't want to see any creature harmed."

Zane nodded. He expected Bowen would be the same. He liked animals.

"So, they set traps, and built a higher fence," Sarah said. "They tried everything. On the last night they put netting on top, too."

"Did it work?" Zane asked, although he suspected he already knew the answer.

"It did," Sarah nodded. "The next day when we came downstairs the chickens were fine. But then I heard Crayf scream. My father tried to stop me, but I ran to her. She was at the rabbit's hutch. There was so much blood. The rabbits were strewn all over the ground like rag dolls."

Zane tried to picture little Sarah, facing that horror.

"My father led me back to the house while Crayf's father held her," Sarah said. "I asked him why the fox would do that. Why would it kill more than it needed to eat? He told me that a tiger can't change its stripes, and that it's a rare creature that can change its nature."

She paused and ran a hand through her hair. "Anyway, that evening we all went to bed, but late in the night I heard a single gunshot."

Zane nodded.

"If Crayf had listened to her father and let him shoot the fox sooner, she wouldn't have lost her rabbits," Sarah said. "Isn't that sad?"

Zane understood her point. And he wanted to explain to her that putting down an animal wasn't like shooting a man. But he didn't think Sarah was of a mind to be explained to just then.

"Whoa, looky here," Slade yelped from just ahead of them.

He had dismounted again and was crouched on the ground with his rump up in the air.

But for some reason, Zane couldn't find it in his heart to find it funny.

He glanced over at Sarah, at the look of determination she wore, and just couldn't shake the foreboding feeling that came over him.

23

SARAH

Sarah half-listened to Slade prattle on about some clue while she kept her eyes on the valley ahead.

She swore she'd seen movement, but with the dim light undulating as the clouds above floated by, it was hard to tell what was real and what was a trick of the light.

"So, what you're saying is we're headed in the right direction?" Zane asked loudly, cutting off whatever Slade was longwindedly explaining.

"Yes," Slade said, getting to his feet and briskly brushing off his breeches. "We're going in precisely the right direction."

She returned her gaze to the meadow ahead, while Slade got back onto his steed.

The clouds had opened up slightly to reveal what she thought she had seen before.

A man, with a young boy by his side, was working with some sort of animal.

"Look," she said. "Maybe they saw something."

"Tumbler flower farmer," Slade said. "They do spend a good bit of time outdoors. Let's find out what they've seen."

As they drew closer, an incredible smell wafted toward them.

"Mmm," Sarah said appreciatively.

"That's the flowers," Slade said, tapping his nose. "They're used for tea and baking, even some perfumes. But they're only good if you harvest the petals at the peak of their bloom. Tricky business."

Before long, they were close enough to realize that the farmers were having trouble.

The man had his back to them. He was pulling the animal's harness as the boy tried to push it from behind. They were surrounded by a sea of flowers with petals so long and soft-looking they were almost like puffy little pompoms.

The boy spotted them and gestured to his father, who turned and waved to them.

"Let me see if I can help," Zane said, dismounting and handing Bowen off to Sarah.

She nodded and pulled the little one into her arms. He immediately grabbed her face in his chubby hands, his mouth forming a tiny "o".

By the time she and Bowen caught up, Zane and Slade were hard at work helping the farmer free his animal.

It was a large, dapple-grey beast, with limpid dark eyes and a fanned tail. She guessed it was more a beast of burden than a mount.

"Howdy, ma'am," the young boy said politely. "Is that your kin rescuing our meadow-seal?"

"They're my traveling companions," she said carefully. "What about that man?"

"That's my Paw," the boy said.

"What happened to your meadow-seal?" she asked.

"Her job is to move rocks and tree branches out of the

way," the boy said solemnly. "But she hit a crick and got stuck."

Sarah understood none of that.

"She moves rocks and tree branches out of the way of what?" she asked.

"The tumbler," the boy said, as if it were the most obvious thing in the world.

He pointed down the field and she saw a large round robot with what looked like combs radiating off it. Fronds of pink petals hung from one of the combs. The saucer-sized colored lights on it told her the tech was ancient enough to be practically run on clockwork.

"It's old, but it has real electrum workings," the boy said proudly. "It'll run forever. That's what my Paw says. But it doesn't have a sensor like the new ones, to move stuff outta the way. That's where Bess comes in."

"Bess is the seal?" Sarah guessed.

"Yep," the boy said. "She's real strong, and smart too. But she got stuck in a crick."

He shook his head sadly and for a moment he looked almost like a little old man.

"What is a crick?" she asked.

"You know," the boy said, unbelieving. "A crick. Like... water coming out of the ground?"

"Oh, of course," she nodded. "Like a creek, or a natural spring."

"That's what I said," he said, looking at her oddly.

Sarah glanced over to see Zane wink at her, his eyes blazing gold instead of blue.

"She won't be stuck for long, I don't think," Sarah told the boy.

Slade counted down and all three men heaved.

It was impossible not to notice Zane's muscles bulging

practically out of his shirt. His jaw was tight with the effort, and Sarah found herself holding her breath as she watched.

At last, the meadow-seal's front legs were released from the muck with a loud sucking sound. The beast clambered away, releasing a trail of petals behind her that hung in the air for a long time before drifting downward.

"Hot damn," the farmer yelled and waded over to clasp arms with Zane. "Feller like you would make a great hand. You lookin' for work?"

"Thank you," Zane said politely. "I'm not looking for work, but I am looking for something. Maybe you can help?"

24

SARAH

Sarah wondered if Zane had asked for help too quickly. Good manners were important.

"I'd be happy to return your favor, but you'll have to tell me about it over lunch," the farmer said. "The name is Bryxx, by the way, and that's my boy, Pyr."

"Good to meet you both," Zane replied. "I'm Zane, that's Slade, and up on the stag-horse is Sarah and her son, Bowen."

"A pleasure," Bryxx said. "Pyr, take them back to the house. I'll just cover this crick and join you."

Zane and Slade retrieved their mounts, and they all followed the boy across the fragrant field to the farmhouse, which stood against the base of a hill. There was a pretty cottage built into the hillside above.

"Maw," the boy shouted at the front door.

"Inside voice now, Pyr," a woman said softly, opening it.

"Maw, these here people helped Paw get Bess out of a crick," Pyr shouted, ignoring her earlier admonition in his excitement. "He says they're to have lunch with us."

The woman gazed out at them suspiciously. But when her eyes found Bowen her face lit up.

"Well then, Pyr, take their mounts and send them in," she scolded him gently. "You're all most welcome."

She waved to them in a friendly way.

Zane dismounted and helped Sarah down with Bowen. By the time they reached the front step along with Slade, the lady of the house was opening the door for them.

"My name is Frylla," she said. "Come on inside."

They stepped into a bright and cheerful living room. However murky the outside was, Frylla and Bryxx seemed determined to combat it inside. There were small blown glass globe lights strung on hooks covering the ceiling and giving the house the feeling of a party.

"Don't mind those," Frylla said, glancing up at the lights. "It's a bit of a hobby."

"You made them?" Sarah asked. The workmanship was excellent. She didn't doubt they would have fetched a handsome price in some of the boutique shops back home.

"In my spare time," Frylla shrugged, turning her attention to Bowen. "Now let's see this little fellow. What's his name?"

"This is Bowen," Sarah said. "And I'm Sarah, that's Zane and over there is Slade."

"Nice to meet you," Frylla said, without taking her eyes off the baby.

Bowen rattled off a series of strange syllables at her and then turned his attention back to the lights, which he waggled his fingers at, like he wanted to touch them.

"Isn't he the most wonderful baby?" Frylla asked. "We were only blessed once, with our Pyr. But he's better than any ten other boys. This one excluded, of course. Did you have him at Lachesis General or Flytown?"

"He's adopted," Sarah said. "I actually just arrived on Lachesis myself a few days ago to meet him."

"Isn't that wonderful?" Frylla said. "You chose each other. It will bring you luck."

"Something smells good, Maw," Pyr said, obviously angling for lunch.

"Yes, yes, your father put short ribs on the embers this morning," Frylla said. "And *someone* baked a cake while you were out in the field."

"Cake," Pyr yelped and dashed off into the kitchen to make sure.

"And that's the bottomless pit you have to look forward to in about eleven years, give or take," Frylla said fondly. "They'll eat you out of house and home."

Frylla's home looked in no danger of anyone actually going without, so Sarah smiled back.

The front door opened and Bryxx strode in.

"Smells good," he announced with pleasure.

"Wash up, and I'll have everything set out in a jiffy," Frylla said. "Sarah, you come with me."

Sarah followed her into a kitchen with a brick floor and pretty wooden cupboards.

Pyr stood over the table, where a beautifully frosted pink cake was displayed on a shiny blue plate.

"Go outside and wash up at the pump with the others," Frylla told her son.

She and Sarah washed up at the kitchen sink and then Frylla gestured for her to sit while she ran plates and silverware out to the dining room.

"I'll help," Sarah said. "Just one-handed."

"You're a keeper," Frylla decided.

A few minutes later, the men were back, and they were all seated at the roughhewn wood table in the dining room, digging into a delicious meal. They ate in companionable silence, and Sarah couldn't remember when she'd had such a delicious meal.

At last, Bryxx leaned back with a contented sigh, his arm resting on his full belly.

"That's better," he said. "Now let's hear what brings you out this way."

"We're searching for a band of men," Slade said. "They would have come through here earlier today."

"We keep to ourselves," Bryxx said with a frown. "This is open country. People here are let be."

"This is something different," Sarah said carefully.

"What do you mean?" Bryxx demanded.

"This is something… dangerous," she replied, glancing at Pyr and not wanting to say more.

Frylla picked up on what was going on at once.

"Pyr," she said. "Look sharp, boy. Go take a nice slice of that cake out to my Bess. She's had a hard day. When you come back, you can have yours."

The boy took off like his life depended on it.

When they heard the kitchen door slam shut behind him, Frylla gestured for Sarah to continue.

"I'm from Terra-7," Sarah explained. "My father and I went to the bank one day and one of those men robbed it. And while he was at it, he killed my father and injured many others, though there was no need for any bloodshed at all." Her voice broke and she had to stop a moment for fear she would cry. "I aim to find him and bring him to justice, for my father's sake and for the sake of any others he would harm in the future."

"Now that's different, Bryxx," Frylla said.

Bryxx was still frowning.

"The marshal here is an expert tracker," Sarah went on,

gesturing to Slade. "He knows exactly which way they went. So you won't be responsible for telling us where to go. But if we knew anything about how many are in their party, and anything they might have said on the way through, that could help us be prepared for whatever we're up against. The more we know in advance, the more likely we can take them without more lives lost."

"Those boys were rude as hell," Bryxx said quietly. "Came thundering across the field with no respect for my property. Spooked Bess something terrible. That's probably why she ended up getting stuck."

Sarah nodded, not daring to speak.

"Said something about a model," Bryxx added. "About bringing liquor back to the model. I have no idea what that meant."

Across the table, Slade's eyes lit up.

"Anyway, that's about all," he said. "It was just two of them, one real big with horns, another with long yellow hair and a gray hat."

"That's very helpful," Slade said. "We are much obliged to you, sir."

"Don't mention it," Bryxx said.

Pyr came blasting back in the front door. "Cake," he sang out.

Frylla laughed and corralled him into helping her with the plates.

"Do you need more hands?" Bryxx asked quietly, leaning forward. "I ain't a bad shot with a powder rifle."

"We're fine," Zane said quickly. "But we appreciate the offer."

Bryxx nodded and leaned back as his wife and son reappeared with the frosted cake, one slice missing from its center.

Sarah watched as they carved off thick slabs of cake and placed a plate before everyone.

The three of them were happy. That much was clear. They worked hard and enjoyed themselves and each other's company. This was what family life was like on the frontier moon.

Sarah thought it seemed like a good life.

She felt a pang in her heart as she thought about what she might be giving up in order to bring Caldwell to justice.

But he had already taken too much. She couldn't leave him free to do more damage.

25

SARAH

Sarah awoke with a start.

She was sitting on the same wooden chair in Frylla's pretty dining room, but Bowen was no longer in her arms.

"Don't worry, dear," Frylla said. "You two were nodding off, so I put him in Pyr's old crib for a good tuck-in."

"Where's everyone else?" Sarah asked, leaping to her feet.

"They said something about taking care of things and coming back for you," Frylla said. "I think it's a good plan. A takedown is no place for a baby. And we're glad to have you."

"They're leaving without me?" Sarah moaned.

She jumped up and ran out the front door before Frylla could even answer, her heartbeat pounding in her ears.

When she saw them saddling up the stag-horses outside of the barn, she was almost weak-kneed with relief.

"Sarah," Zane said, looking guilty and disappointed at the same time.

"How could you?" she demanded. "How could you try to leave me behind?"

"He was right," Slade said, stepping between them. "A takedown is no place for a baby. And if things go wrong, Bowen will need his mama."

"No," Sarah said. "Absolutely not. I walked away from everything I've ever known to bring him down. I will not be left behind."

"Sarah—" Slade began.

"—*I hired you*," she said. "I'm paying you good money. And you're trying to trick me. I won't have it."

His face fell and he glanced over at Zane, as if for help.

Fury filled Sarah's chest until she couldn't speak.

"Sarah, I have an idea," Frylla's voice was calm and gentle behind her. "Why don't you at least let us keep an eye on Bowen for you? Maybe that would make everyone feel better?"

She turned back to the other woman to argue, but the wind was out of her sails.

Frylla was right, of course. They all were. The battlefield was no place for the boy. But that still didn't give anyone the right to leave her behind.

She nodded, even as tears prickled her eyes at the realization that she might never see her boy again if things didn't go her way.

"Do you want to go say goodbye before you saddle up?" Frylla asked.

Sarah shook her head.

"Then I won't hug you goodbye, because I'm going to see you again real soon," Frylla said. "You go get that man. Kick his ass."

Sarah grinned at her through her tears while Zane saddled up her mount.

Frylla waved and headed back to the house.

Zane tried to meet Sarah's eye as he led the stag-mare up to her. But she took the reins without giving him the satisfaction.

Mate for life, my ass, she thought to herself. *You were ready to betray me at the first opportunity.*

"Sarah, I only want to protect you," he murmured.

"Don't be condescending," she said crisply. "It demeans us both."

She clucked to the mare before he could argue, and set off across the meadow.

26

ZANE

Zane looked on from behind as Sarah rode in silence, just a little too quickly for Zane's staghorse to match her rhythm.

He could feel the pain radiating off her, and he couldn't blame her for being angry.

But could she blame him for wanting to protect her?

"Sarah," he called to her.

She ignored him.

"Sarah, please. You need to know where we're headed, and what we're going to find," he said. "Will you allow me to tell you what Slade figured out from Bryxx's info?"

She slowed down and let him catch up.

The relief he felt was almost overwhelming.

But Sarah didn't meet his eyes, merely allowing him to trot alongside.

"When Bryxx said *the model*, that didn't mean anything to me," Zane said. "But Slade knew immediately. They're at that half-built housing development."

"Lachesis Valley?" Sarah asked. "The one the guy was giving out brochures for in the town square?"

"Good memory," Zane said. "Yes, that's the one."

"So, they're hiding out in the model home," Sarah said thoughtfully.

"Sounds that way," Zane said. "Slade says it's at the center of the thing, so we'll have to sneak up on it."

He looked around them. The meadows had already given way to mud and marsh.

"It's dangerous out here," he went on. "Rough terrain, and Slade says it's worse there."

She nodded once.

"Sarah, I'm sorry," he said. "I only wanted to save you."

"I don't need saving," she said. "Now if you'll excuse me, I need to clear my head. I've waited a long time for this."

He nodded and let her get ahead of him again.

The ground grew wetter as they went, the stag-horses' feet making sticky sounds as they traversed the muck. Before long, Sarah stopped suddenly ahead of him.

"What's wrong?" he asked.

"This mud, it's too thick," she said. "Remember the seal? Will our mounts get stuck?"

"Let me get ahead of you a bit so you can see their hooves," he replied as he rode his horse out.

"Oh, wow," she said. "Their hooves are webbed."

"They come from this kind of terrain," he agreed. "The split hoof with webbing helps them travel the marshes without getting stuck.

"Amazing," Sarah said, pulling confidently ahead once more.

They traveled on in silence, the light mist along the land growing thicker until they could see only a few meters in any direction.

Somewhere up ahead, a ghostly moan emerged from the mist.

"Sarah," Zane called.

To her credit, she pulled her mount up to wait for him.

Slade brought his stallion up and joined Zane as they traversed the misty marsh to find the source of the sound.

The sound grew louder and suddenly they were looking down at a familiar beggars-mule, sunk chest deep in the muck. The beast had belonged to the men they were following. It struggled in terror when it saw them, eyes rolling back in its head until they could only see the whites.

"His leg," Slade muttered.

Zane had smelled the blood. The poor creature had shattered a rear leg trying to free itself.

"Zane?" Sarah called from behind, her voice was fearful.

"It's okay," he called back to her. "Just a beast stuck in the mud."

She joined them, her pale stag-horse picking its way neatly through the marsh.

"Oh no," she said, her face falling when she saw the unfortunate creature.

"It's alright," Slade said. "I'll take care of it. You two go on."

Zane nodded to him, grateful to the marshal for being subtle for once.

"Come, Sarah," Zane said.

They continued through the mist.

"Do you really think he'll be able to get it out of the mud alone?" Sarah asked Zane. "Shouldn't you help him?"

Before he could reply, a single gunshot rang out across the marsh.

A moment later they could hear the soggy squish of hoofbeats heading their way.

"All taken care of," Slade said, a solemn expression on his face.

"You- you killed it," Sarah said.

"Its rear leg was shattered," Slade said. "It was a goner. Poor thing would have drowned, if its heart didn't burst in terror first. If those cowards we're after had half a heart between them, they'd have done it themselves."

Zane watched as Sarah buttoned her lip and urged her mount on, her back stiff and straight, clearly rattled by the idea.

He tried to focus on catching up and keeping her in his sight. But he couldn't stop his mind from reeling. Her innocence would end up being her undoing. She couldn't even stand knowing that a lame mule had been put out of its misery.

Killing another human being would destroy her.

27

SARAH

It was full dark by the time they reached the edges of the development. If not for the soft glow of starlight peeking through the clouds, Sarah wouldn't have been able to see at all.

The facades of the buildings made strange shapes against the slate-gray sky. From what she could make out, there were two sets of townhouses, separated by a little hill with a stand of scraggly trees.

The row on the right was clearly sinking into the bog. Fingers of algae reached out of the murky water to pull at the rough wooden walls. Doors and windows were popping out as the buildings were pulled askew on their journey downward.

As they drew closer, Sarah spotted a dark shape moving under the shallow water that already filled an algae-coated kitchen. She suppressed a shudder and hoped they wouldn't have an opportunity to find out what it was.

"The model is on the other side," Slade pointed out. "It's not as bad over there."

Sarah couldn't imagine the idea of living anywhere near

this half-sunken ghost town. But clearly Caldwell cared more about enabling his degenerate lifestyle than about cleanliness, or spookiness.

"We'll leave the horses here," Slade said, riding up onto the relatively solid ground of the trees between the two sides of the development.

Sarah swung down from her mount, scratching the creature behind her beautiful antlers and accepting a snuffly kiss. This time, she had remembered to save a bit of cake from lunch, and she fed it to the pretty creature before leaving her to join the men.

Together, they looked out over the more stable half of the development.

From her vantage point, Sarah could see that the fronts of the homes were just facades, with the rest of the exteriors constructed of unfinished wood that already had coats of moss growing on them like fur.

Massive construction vehicles, and a huge metal tank that must have been meant to store drinking water, were lined up along the higher side of the development.

Light emanated from just one house, directly at the center. Smoke trailed out of a ragged hole in its roof, as if someone had built a campfire in the main room.

"That's the model," Slade said, pointing to it. "It will be tough to take them as long as they're inside."

"We could smoke them out," Zane suggested.

"Good," Slade said. "You afraid of heights?"

Zane raised an eyebrow.

"Of course," Slade said. "You cover the hole to trap the smoke inside, and I'll find a good point to get the drop on them when they come out."

"What about me?" Sarah asked.

"You stand watch," Slade said. "If anyone leaves the

house before we get up there, whistle and then hide in the trees. You got that? Do not engage with them. We've got them backed into a corner now. Like any trapped creature, they're liable to bite."

Sarah nodded. She knew that she wasn't as skilled as the marshal, but she was determined to do her part rounding up the men.

And when Caldwell finally showed himself, all she needed was to surprise him with one good stab from the sword in her cane.

Zane moved to her, putting a big hand on her shoulder.

"Are you sure you're okay with this?" he asked her. "You don't have to be here. I'll put you back on that stag-mare and send you back to Frylla to wait for us."

"This is what I was meant for," she replied, meeting his eyes and refusing to back down.

"Be careful, Sarah," he said. It sounded like a surrender.

"You too," she told him, nodding.

Slade tipped his hat to her and then they were off, moving slowly and carefully as they approached the model home.

Sarah moved a little closer too, so she could get a view through one of the big windows. It was dark out, and with the fire inside the house, she was sure no one would see her.

Inside the house, the man with the dirty yellow hair was feeding chair legs into a fire pit they had made out of a bathtub. His horned companion watched him, taking swings from a silver canister.

She dared another step closer to see if she could lay eyes on Caldwell.

Something made a huffing sound just past the houses in the area near the construction equipment.

She turned to see a beggars-mule, like the one they'd

passed with the broken leg, tied up to a post. She figured it must belong to Caldwell. She thought about the idea that these men had lost a beast like this in the swamp and just left it to drown. No creature deserved that kind of treatment.

Fury filled her heart, and she marched up to the unfortunate creature, intending to set it free so the villains couldn't get away, even if they somehow managed to sneak past Slade and Zane. And so the beast would never have to suffer at the hands of such thoughtless men.

But before she could reach the post, movement caught her eye from the water just beyond.

A tall, skinny man was standing in the ankle-deep water, watching her. He carried a wooden pike across his back like a yolk, a dozen or more dead, frog-like creatures dangling from it. He was bedraggled and dirty, but she would know that face anywhere.

"Jericho Caldwell," Sarah murmured.

"Who the hell are you?" he asked in a raspy, cigarillo voice.

Sarah's entire universe held its breath as she faced him down, unbelieving.

He coughed once and then just stood there, dripping and staring at her. "You're pretty enough. Did you come here to get some, girl?"

This was the man who had ruined her life.

And he didn't even recognize her.

She whipped her sword out of her cane in a single, beautiful motion, the silver of it gleaming under the stars.

She had thought long and hard about what she might say to this man when she finally caught up to him.

You killed the best man who ever lived.

And here you are, a disgusting, slimy man, in a disgusting, slimy place.

But I'm going to send you somewhere you can burn.

The words were loud in her head, but the only thing that came out when she opened her mouth was an inhuman war scream.

Caldwell flinched backward, as if he finally understood that she was an angel of justice who had come to collect her prize.

Sarah moved fast, her skirts billowing as she ran at him, sword aimed for his black heart.

But Caldwell stepped back at the last second and she sailed past him. The sword made a nasty slash on his arm on the way by, but did not hit its mark.

"You fucking bitch," Caldwell screamed.

He spun, hitting her hard in the head with the wooden pike.

Sarah felt the impact before the pain, felt herself flying, felt the soggy ground move up to catch her.

Cold thick mud filled her shoes and clothing and pulled at her skin. Then the pain landed on her like an anvil and she nearly suffocated under its weight.

The world grew dim around the edges of her vision, but she could hear Caldwell's lazy footsteps moving toward her through the muck.

She tried to scream, but the sound was covered by a barrage of gunshots coming from the model home.

28

ZANE

Zane waited for the signal from Slade, and then pulled his stag-horse's riding blanket over the hole in the model home's roof. He tried to ensure it covered the area completely, without going close enough for the compromised roof structure to give way under his weight.

Slade was squatting at the far edge of the roof, just over the front door, ready to aim at anyone who ran outside.

Once the blanket was fully in place, Zane waited, hoping Sarah had done as she promised and stayed close. He didn't like leaving her alone, and less so in this place. The bog was dangerous of its own accord, even without the den of vicious criminals.

"Here we go," Slade muttered as the door below banged open.

Zane turned his attention back the to the marshal and the front of the building.

Coughs and cursing wafted up to them as the men tumbled out of the model home, hunched over and looking miserable.

But there were only two of them - the two they'd been following. No sign of Caldwell, or anyone else.

Before Zane had time to even scan the area, the big Maltaffian wheeled, pulling two blasters out of his jacket.

Gunshots rent the air.

Slade rolled for cover along the far side of the roof as the second villain pulled out a rifle and fired wildly in their general direction.

"I am a duly appointed officer of the law," Slade announced. "This is your final chance to surrender peacefully."

The only answer was more gunfire, as the men below scrambled for cover.

"Then it looks like we'll do it the hard way," Slade said with a wild grin as he peeked up and returned fire.

More shots rang out all around, but Zane paid them no mind. His thoughts were focused on one thing.

Sarah.

The marshal could clearly handle himself with those two. But if they decided to make a run for it, they might bump into Sarah. And if Caldwell really was around here somewhere...

He sprinted across the rooftop and looked down on the spot where he had left his mate, but she was nowhere to be seen.

He closed his eyes and lifted his nose to the air, searching for her scent.

The dragon clawed for the surface, ready to take over his body, but he needed to keep his wits about him.

Not yet, he told it. *Find her.*

The dragon inhaled and a world of smells swirled all around him, so intense they were almost like colors. The blue-green of the trees, the brown of the bog.

And then, faintly, from the direction of the swamp, the lavender mist that was his Sarah.

He opened his eyes and surveyed the area, deciding he could get there faster on the rooftops than the wet ground. He took a running leap onto the roof of the next house, landing hard on his haunches.

He knocked a few shingles loose, but the roofing held, and he sucked in a breath before taking a run at the next one.

It held his weight too, and he ran for all he was worth and landed on the roof of a smaller outbuilding, then finally lowered himself to the ground.

He heard a muffled scream coming from the bog up ahead.

"Sarah," he groaned, running for her.

Her face was barely above the water. Zane bent to her and cradled her head in his arms.

"Are you hurt, or can I get you up?" he asked.

"I'm fine," she said, grabbing onto his shoulders to try to pull herself up and out of the muck.

"Sarah," he said, noting the marks on her head and neck.

"Stop worrying about me," she yelled, her voice tinged with despair. "He's getting away."

Zane looked up just in time to spot the tall, thin man running away in the direction of the construction equipment.

29

SARAH

Sarah let her fingers sink into Zane's shoulders, desperate for him to help her chase down Caldwell.

She saw the exact moment when he noticed Caldwell running for the hills.

Zane seemed to wake up, grabbing her and wrenching her out of the muck.

She flung herself forward before she even caught her breath, stumbling and then catching herself as she ran, pumping her legs to keep her feet under herself as she went full tilt.

She had no idea what was under the water beneath her feet, or what obstacles lay ahead, and she didn't care. In the dim starlight filtering through the clouds, she could barely keep her eyes on the only thing that mattered - the lanky form of Jericho Caldwell.

Zane's big footsteps thundered behind her, catching up quickly. Then his hand was warm around hers, and she knew he wouldn't let her fall.

Within seconds, they were gaining on Caldwell, his footsteps echoed on what must be rocks or pavement. The going was faster once they were out of the soggy mud of the marsh.

But before they could get a hand on him, Caldwell ducked around a corner and she lost sight of him.

Zane half-dragged her with him and they came out on the other side of a half-built wall.

Caldwell was nowhere in sight.

"Come on," Zane murmured, as if he could taste her despair.

They backtracked a bit, slipping behind some boards and back out into the open.

Sarah looked around, frantic.

Zane squeezed her hand, and she looked in the direction of his gaze.

Caldwell was sitting above them, in the cab of an enormous piece of machinery. It was as big as a planetary gadabout, with a giant crane arm coming off the cab.

Caldwell glowered at them from behind the bubble of glass. Then the engine revved to life, red warning lights flashing.

There was no time to think. One minute Sarah was trying to figure out what was happening. The next, Caldwell sank the pedal to the metal and the engine whined. Acrid smoke filled the air as the treads tried to find purchase in the marshy ground. Then it was lurching toward them, the crane arm swinging wildly.

Zane pulled her back, and they hit the boards behind them hard enough to rattle her teeth. Before they could try to run, the crane arm smashed into the gigantic metal tank she'd spotted earlier.

The water tank rang out like a gong and crashed onto its side, rolling toward Sarah and Zane.

It was moving too fast, and they were pinned in place.

We're going to die. What will happen to Bowen?

Clarity descended on her in a blinding flash.

Everything she had done since arriving on this moon had been wrong.

She heard her father's voice in her head.

It is a rare creature that can change its nature.

Sarah's nature was not to be a killer. And she didn't want that to change.

Jericho Caldwell could have escaped, but he wasn't satisfied with that. He wanted to hurt them first.

She was nothing like the man in the cab of that crane, and she didn't ever want to be.

She wanted to teach Bowen better - to be sure he knew right from wrong, just as her father raised her.

But it was too late now. She and Zane were about to die.

30

SARAH

Sarah closed her eyes and felt the air around her shivering.

That wasn't right.

She opened them again to see that Zane was moving forward to shove his shoulder against the tank.

One moment he was a man, muscles bulging against the unstoppable force.

The next, he was a dragon, scales shimmering in the hazy starlight, towering over her.

The dragon snorted and gave the tank a shove. It shot out into the swamp, thundering and splashing its way to a stop.

But now there was nothing between them and the crane machine.

Caldwell revved the engine, sending the machine hurtling forward as he swung the crane right at the dragon's face.

The dragon roared, flames shooting out of its mouth.

A wall of heat pushed outward, lifting Sarah's hair.

She watched in awe as the fire hit the crane. The massive

metal arm melted mid-swing, molten steel dripping to the boggy ground before it could touch them.

Caldwell immediately flung himself out of the cab, and darted away as fast as his feet would carry him.

But even his fastest was far too slow.

The dragon was on him in an instant, pinning him down with a single golden claw.

Caldwell moaned in fear, the sound high pitched and reedy thin, like fingernails on a chalkboard. A dark stain spread along the seams of his trousers as his terror got the better of him.

The dragon let his golden head fall back so that Sarah could see the smaller and more exquisite scales on the underside of his neck. He inhaled a breath that made his great chest swell.

Sarah realized what was happening at the last second.

He's going to kill him.

She pictured the crane arm melting under that intense heat and suddenly her feet were moving.

"Zane, *no*," she cried, throwing her body over Caldwell's.

The dragon roared and blew his flames straight up into the air instead.

And though the blast of heat reminded her how dangerous it was, the blossom of flames was also undeniably beautiful.

It billowed into the low clouds of Lachesis, lighting them up like fireworks.

31

ZANE

Zane pushed his way to the front of the dragon's mind, but he was still shaking with fury as he emerged in his own form, his strong hand locked around Caldwell's throat.

Sarah blinked up at him from her position across Caldwell's chest, as if surprised herself at what she had done.

Under his grip, Caldwell made a choking sound and struggled weakly.

"Let him breathe, Zane," Sarah said softly, scrambling off the villain.

"He could have run," Zane roared, tightening his grip. "He could have gotten into that thing and just driven away."

Caldwell's eyes were bugging out beneath him. If he thought he was going to get kinder treatment from the man than the beast, he was sadly mistaken. His Sarah might not be made for such violence, but he was.

"But he didn't run," Zane went on, the words harsh with so much rage he almost didn't recognize his own voice. "He tried to kill you."

"Zane," Sarah murmured.

"You were right," Zane snapped. "He's the fox in the story. He's never going to change his ways. But I can end it right now. I can make sure he never hurts anyone else again."

Caldwell began to struggle again in earnest as Zane's intent became clear.

"No," Sarah pleaded.

"No?" Zane asked, looking up at her. "What do you mean *no*?"

"He *is* the fox," she said. "But I'm not a killer. And neither are you. We are about to start a new life together with our son. We can't begin that on a foundation of death and revenge."

Our son...

His white-hot rage retreated slightly, making room for hope.

We are about to start a new life together...

He removed his hand from Caldwell's neck and grabbed the man's wrists, hauling him shakily to his feet as Slade came into view, leading two handcuffed prisoners of his own.

"You got one, eh?" Slade's cocky tone didn't seem as obnoxious as usual to Zane.

"He nearly killed us," Sarah explained.

"But he didn't," Slade pointed out. "And after that little pyrotechnic display, I expected to find him nothing more than a pile of ashes and bad decisions."

"We want him alive," Sarah said. "We want him to answer for his crimes in court, and live with the consequences of his actions. Can you promise me you'll do your best to see to it that he isn't let off?"

"I promise you, ma'am," Slade said solemnly. "He will not leave my sight until he's behind bars."

Sarah nodded, clearly satisfied with his assurance.

Zane watched her closely as Slade cuffed Caldwell and read him his rights.

There was no trace of regret on her face. She seemed to be at peace.

"There's another mule tied up in the trees," Sarah said. "We should bring it, too."

Slade nodded and urged his prisoners forward in front of him.

"What made you change your mind?" Zane asked Sarah when there was enough distance between them for privacy.

"You were right all along," she told him. "What I was planning was vengeance."

He nodded, not wanting to agree, but knowing she was right.

"But what I really wanted was justice," she said. "Seeing how Slade treats his job makes me think it is possible to get justice on Lachesis."

"True," Zane said begrudgingly. Whatever else he might think about the marshal, the man was fair, and good at his job.

"And I'd rather spend the rest of my life trying to find justice in the courts, than become a killer myself," she said. "It was one thing when it seemed like vengeance was all I had, but I have too much to live for now."

Zane stopped in his tracks.

Even though it was cold, and they were both covered in bog mud, he grabbed her by the shoulders and pressed his lips to hers.

Sarah went up on her toes, winding her arms around his neck and kissing him back in an embrace that was hungry, passionate, and filled with promise.

32

SARAH

A few hours later, Sarah and Zane watched from the lawn in front of the farmhouse, as Slade greeted the other marshal he'd called in for backup.

The journey back through the wetlands with their prisoners had been arduous, but it felt good to be this close to Bowen and a good night's sleep.

Caldwell and the others were still cuffed and compliant, but Sarah was glad that Slade had someone else on hand to get them safely to the town jail.

She hadn't been looking forward to traveling with her son and her father's killer all the way back to town. Now Slade didn't need Zane along to keep things under control.

Not that Slade would have admitted he needed help in the first place. The marshal was nothing if not confident.

Slade looked up at her as if she had called to him, and waved, then began jogging her way.

"Sarah," he said with a smile as soon as he reached them. "You have my word that I'll see him brought to justice."

"I know that's not in your power, Slade," she told him gently. "But thank you for doing all you can."

She pulled her pouch from her pocket and handed it to him. "There are two thousand credits in there. Count it."

"Don't have to," he said, slipping it into his breast pocket and patting it in a satisfied way. "Thank you."

"Thank *you*," she told him. "Your tracking skills got us our man."

"When we get back to town, I'll send word to Terra-7," he said. "They'll send evidence. And maybe you'll testify?"

"Of course I will," Sarah said. "About what happened at the bank, and about last night."

"So will I," Zane said, his deep voice solemn.

"Much obliged to both of you," Slade said, tipping his cap. "Maybe see you in town sometime?"

He gave Sarah an appraising glance, as if maybe he was asking more than he seemed to be asking.

She could feel Zane bristle through their bond.

"Maybe we will," she told him, emphasizing the *we* ever so slightly.

Slade gave her a warm smile of understanding.

"You're a lucky fella," he told Zane. "Don't mess it up."

Zane only glared at him.

Slade laughed and thumped him on the shoulder. "You're alright, dragon man."

He headed back down to his partner and the prisoner, clearly excited about bringing in his quarry, plus the two bonus arrests that came along with it.

"Cocky bastard," Zane muttered.

"Zane, are you... jealous?" she asked.

He snorted, but his golden cheeks blushed a burnished copper.

"Let's go get our son," she told him.

He wrapped his hand around hers and they went to the house.

Sarah knocked on the door with trembling hands.

"Oh, thank heavens," Frylla cried, pulling Sarah into a warm embrace.

"There they are," Bryxx's voice rang out from the dining room.

He appeared a moment later with Bowen in his arms.

The little one reached for Zane, and for a moment, Sarah's feelings were just a little bit hurt.

Then she saw the smile on her mate's handsome face, and all was forgotten.

"*Bah*," Bowen cried and smacked Zane on the chest.

"Hello, little one," Zane said.

Bowen squeaked back at him and then reached for Sarah.

She came close and let him take her face in his small hands.

For once, he was very gentle, his fingers soft against her face, his eyes wide. He leaned close and touched his forehead to hers as Zane held him with one arm and wrapped the other around her.

Bowen's sweet scent filled her senses and Sarah felt something akin to euphoria settle over her in the embrace of the two people she loved most.

She forgot they were in someone else's living room, covered in mud and completely exhausted. She forgot all the sadness and struggle that had brought them together. Sarah Flynn breathed in the love of her family and felt like a princess.

"Now, it's late," Bryxx said. "And you've had quite a day. Frylla had a thought."

"We've already got Pyr's old crib set up for your wee

one," Frylla said. "And there's no one in the guest house. Why don't you stay a few days? We'll look after the little one."

"A few *days*?" Sarah echoed.

"We know the beginning of a relationship can be... intense with Zane's kind," Frylla said, studying her shoes very carefully as she spoke.

"Intense?" Sarah repeated, looking to Zane.

"Surely you told her," Frylla said to Zane in a shocked way.

"I'll explain on the way to the guest house," Zane told her. "If you'd like to stay?"

"Sure," she said, still trying to understand.

"We took the liberty of stocking the pantry over there," Frylla said with a smile. "But let us know if you need anything."

Bowen let out a mighty yawn.

"Yes, sweet boy," Frylla crooned. "Come with Auntie Frylla. It's time for sleeping."

Bowen went to her happily, without even a backward glance.

"Let's go," Zane growled.

"Have fun, you two," Bryxx said, stepping forward to drop a key in her hand.

"Thank you," she said, closing her hand around the little fob.

Then she was being swept up into Zane's powerful arms and carried out the door.

33

ZANE

Zane placed Sarah down on the floor of the cottage and looked around.

He realized there must be better money in tumbler flower farming than he had previously thought.

Though the farmhouse had been a sprawling old-fashioned construction, meant to mimic the farmhouses of old Earth, this little cottage had some top of the line technological amenities.

The LED ceiling was currently displaying a starry sky, similar to the real one outside, only without the cloud cover. A top of the line scentillator made the space smell like a meadow in springtime, but it could not cover the sweet scent of his mate.

"You smell so good," he murmured.

"I need a bath," she whispered back.

He laughed and she smiled up at him. He wouldn't have cared if she had just crawled through crab-duck manure to get here, he would have taken her just as she was.

But he wanted her to be comfortable. They were going to be here a while.

"Why don't I start you a bath and explain about everything?" he offered.

"I'd like that," she agreed.

The bathroom was nearly filled by a giant tub. A tiny stall shower and the other necessaries seemed to be there as an afterthought. He rummaged through the linen closet, hoping to find a bottle of bubbly stuff for the bath.

"That tub looks amazing," Sarah sighed. "But maybe I'd better shower off the worst of it first."

He shrugged.

"Turn your back, please," she said, suddenly demure.

He grinned at her and turned his back, shaking his head.

Soon, she wouldn't cover herself from him. He would make her see how beautiful she was to him. She would preen and strut by the end of this night.

He could hear the shower water turn on and couldn't resist sneaking a quick peek.

The sight of clean rivulets of water uncovering her tender flesh from under a coating of mud was satisfying and strangely sexy.

He turned back to the bath, hoping she hadn't caught him looking.

"Ahh," she moaned.

He clenched his fists by his sides. "You doing okay over there?" he asked. "Need any help?"

"Nope, almost done," she said. "It just feels so good not to be caked in mud."

That did sound pretty good.

He began stripping off his clothes, too. No reason to ruin a nice bubble bath with a layer of mud.

"Oh," she said.

He turned to find that she had stepped out of the shower. She was perfectly naked and absolutely ravishing.

"I, uh, was going to shower off too," he told her.

She nodded, staring at his abs and then allowing her eyes to drop lower.

He felt his body respond to her gaze, throbbing for her.

Her lips parted and he very nearly lost control.

But he would not claim her until she begged.

"Okay for me to step in there?" he asked, indicating the shower.

She stepped out of the way, still looking a little dazed, and he stepped past her into the heat of the shower.

The hot water felt incredible against his skin. He lathered up soap and ran it all over his body and hair, then stood under the hot spray to rinse. He'd been on plenty of worlds where water was scarce, and a shower like this would have been impossible. He was glad water was plentiful on this little frontier moon.

When he opened his eyes, he saw Sarah was still standing in front of the shower, watching him.

Claim her. Now, the dragon roared in his chest.

He froze in place, fighting for control.

"Zane," Sarah murmured. "I need you."

He was out of the shower in a flash, lifting her in his arms and carrying her to the bedroom.

She didn't protest, not even when he threw her on the bed and climbed in after her, caging her head in his arms, pinning her naked body to the mattress with his own.

She lifted her face for a kiss, with an impetuous air that made him wild.

Yes, you are mine. Yes, you will have my kiss. But not yet, the dragon crooned.

"Wait," Zane managed, through gritted teeth. "I need to explain."

"Please hurry," she whispered.

He pressed his forehead to hers, praying for strength.

"When a dragon claims his mate, the joining can go on for days," he told her.

"For days?"

"We won't want to leave this cottage," he told her. "Maybe we won't even want to leave the bed. It's going to be intense. And once we're joined, it's forever."

"I understand," she said softly.

He pulled back to meet her eyes.

"I'm ready," she assured him.

"Ready for days in bed together?" he asked. "Or ready for forever?"

"Both," she said with a sly smile.

The word sent a lightning bolt of joy through his heart and he bent to kiss her sweet lips.

34

SARAH

Sarah's heart pounded as he kissed her, thundering so loudly she was afraid it would leave her chest.

There was a feeling just under her skin, a restlessness that demanded him, demanded something... something beyond the indulgent satisfaction she had tasted with him before.

This time she craved the darkness of the bond, and the needs of his body as well as her own.

He pulled back slightly, and she tried to lift herself to meet his mouth again.

But he tangled his hand in her hair and held her firm.

"Zane," she murmured.

But he held her fast, pressing his lips to her neck, and then lower to nuzzle her breasts.

The pleasure was building in her already. She clung to the sheets as though she might be swept away.

Zane licked one nipple into his mouth and stroked the other lightly with his fingers.

Sarah moaned and arched her back.

He growled against her breast and fed on her desperately.

She could feel him, rigid against her thigh, and her insides clenched, even as she wondered how she could possibly take him in.

"Zane," she moaned.

He pressed kisses against her belly, rubbing his rough jaw against the tender flesh, moving slowly, so slowly.

Sarah felt as if her whole body was on fire and Zane's touch was the only thing that would bring her peace. She wanted him to touch every part of her at once, to fill her pores and occupy her mind.

Instead, he brushed her trembling flesh with his lips and scraped her with his teeth, giving her just enough teasing contact to stop her from dying, but not enough to fill her needs.

She whimpered as he pressed kisses to her inner thighs.

"Easy, my love," he whispered, his hot breath moving through her curls to tease her needy sex.

She nearly screamed, but then he was parting her with his fingers, flooding her with shivers of desire.

The first touch of his tongue sent a shock of almost unbearable pleasure through her.

Then he set to work, licking her slowly, each firm stroke of his tongue ending with a tiny flick against her most sensitive spot.

Sarah wailed and lifted her hips, but he only slowed his movements, pushing her closer and closer.

"Please," she moaned. "Please, Zane, please..."

He pulled back and then he was crawling up to her, pinning her to the bed once more.

This time the magnificent throbbing of his cock against her belly didn't frighten her.

She ached for him, needed him more than she needed her next breath. There was nothing he could do to her that would hurt more than his absence from her body hurt her right now.

"Are you ready, Sarah?" he asked her, fixing her with his blue eyes, which she swore shimmered now with iridescent gold. "Will you accept me as your mate?"

"Yes," she moaned.

"Mine," he growled, plunging his length inside her.

She felt her body stretch to accommodate him. Pain quickly gave way to yawning pleasure.

"Please," she moaned, tilting her hips to urge him on.

"Gods, Sarah," he murmured through his clenched jaw. "You feel so good, too good."

"Please, please, please," she whined shamelessly wiggling her hips frantically.

"Fuck," he groaned and plunged again.

She clung to him, as the pleasure nearly sent her out of her mind.

He thrust again and again, as if he had abandoned his quest to tease her to distraction, as if he were chasing his own pleasure now.

She could feel it through their bond, his need was rough and desperate, the perfect counterpoint to her own.

"Please," she whispered.

He slid a hand between them and massaged her as he thrust again.

The ecstasy splintered her, she felt herself flying outward in sparkling pieces as Zane shouted out his own pleasure, jetting inside her again and again.

At last the pleasure floated her down again and Zane fell on her chest, panting and pressing kisses to her breasts.

There was something different, a tension in the tiny spaces between them that shivered like magnetism.

"The bond," she whispered in wonder. "I can feel it."

"I can feel it too," he told her. "Are you thirsty or hungry?"

"Not yet," she said. "Let's rest a while."

He chuckled.

"What?" she asked.

"We don't have a while," he murmured, nuzzling her neck. "As a matter of fact, I'm not even sure we have a minute."

"That's impossible," she said.

But she already felt the pull of longing blossoming up again, making her moan with the need for him to claim her.

"Easy, my love," he murmured. "I've got you."

She closed her eyes and gave in to desire.

35

SARAH

A week later, Sarah worked outside in the garden of her own home, while Bowen relaxed on a blanket beside her, squeaking at the butterflies that floated past.

A bit more light than usual filtered through the cloud cover, lightening the saturated hues of the trees and grass and showing off the baby's golden shimmer.

Zane was inside cooking up a big brunch for them.

When the mating thrall had finally loosened its hold long enough for the two of them to eat, the golden warrior had discovered that he liked the clay oven at Bryxx and Frylla's cottage.

Now that they were home again, he had bought one for himself and the house always seemed to be filled with the smells of his latest cooking experiment. No one was more excited than Zane about the big Intermoon Market that was coming to Lachesis soon, with spices and other delicacies from all over the galaxy. They were planning a big potluck with their friends on the farm, replete with all kinds of exotic offerings.

Zane had even let her know where his Invicta brothers had ended up settling with her friends from the adoption process, and they had sent word, inviting the other couples to join them as well. It would be nice to catch up with the other adoptive mothers and see how they were doing.

As for Sarah, she was allowing herself a little time to get to know her son and her new home. The days were happy, filled with reading and singing and outside time with Bowen.

And the nights with Zane were incredible.

After years of sadness about the past, Sarah was finally focused on the future. It felt good.

"*Bah*," Bowen yelled, waving his chubby arms in the direction of the street.

Sarah looked up to see a familiar man on an ink black stag-stallion, galloping their way.

"Slade," she called out, scooping Bowen up in her arms and walking over to greet their friend.

"Howdy, Sarah," Slade said, hopping off his mount and wrapping its harness around one of the wooden posts in front of the house.

"It's good to see you," she told him. "Is everything okay?"

"Everything is more than okay," he told her. "Is your dragon man around? I'd love to see how you two are settling in, and share a little news."

"Of course," Sarah said. "He's inside. I hope you're hungry."

"I could eat," Slade said with a wolfish grin.

She headed to the door and threw it open, releasing the scent of berry cakes, bacon, and coffee.

"Oh sweet Lord," Slade said appreciatively. "You must have been cooking all morning."

"Not me," Sarah said.

"Slade," Zane called to him happily.

Sarah let her focus move to their bond, testing.

There was no jealousy there anymore, only joy at seeing their mutual friend.

She let him feel her own happiness through the bond as well. It was good to have a shared friend. He was right not to feel threatened. Slade might be a flirt, but Sarah and Zane were mates. Nothing would ever come between them.

"Buddy, did you make all this?" Slade asked.

"Sure did," Zane said. "Grab a plate. You want coffee?"

"I'll get the coffee," Sarah offered.

Bowen yelled out a few syllables too, exited to be part of the conversation.

"Good thinking, son," Zane told him. "We'll fix you some milk."

Slade sat down at one of the stools and watched them bustle around.

"Any chance the little fella would let Uncle Slade hold him?" he offered.

"I'll bet he would," Sarah said, carrying Bowen over.

He put his arms out to Slade immediately, and the marshal took him, a delighted expression on his face.

Bowen immediately began trying to pluck the golden badge off Slade's uniform.

"Oh, you want to be a marshal too, huh?" Slade asked him.

Bowen laughed and tugged at Slade's hair instead of his badge.

Sarah set a mug of coffee down in front of him, just out of reach of Bowen's chubby hands, then poured a cup each for herself and Zane.

Zane plated out berry cakes, bacon, and an egg bake for each of them, and then prepared Bowen's bottle.

"I'll take him," he told Slade when the bottle was ready. "You eat while it's hot."

"No, man, you cooked," Slade said.

"He likes to cook," Sarah said. "Besides, I'm anxious to know your news."

"Ah," Slade said. "In that case..."

He handed the baby to Zane and took a sip of coffee, his eyes lighting up. "Delicious. That's one of the worst parts of this moon. No one around here knows how to make a decent cup of coffee. But this tastes just like home."

"Thanks," Zane said.

"So, I guess you're wondering what's happening with Jericho Caldwell?" Slade asked.

Sarah nodded, not wanting to waste time with a *yes.*

"Turns out, once we did a retinal scan, we found out he's got a few more aliases," Slade said. "That man is wanted all over the sector."

"I'm not surprised," Sarah said. "A man like that doesn't start doing evil out of nowhere."

"Right you are, little lady," Slade said, tapping the side of his nose. "He's left behind a trail of violence and loss. The only good news is, he's going to pay for it. Right now, our biggest challenge is in-fighting among the jurisdictions that want a hand in this. At least it was."

"What do you mean *it was,*" Sarah asked.

Please, don't let him have escaped...

"I say *was* because the latest call our office got was a personal holo from Ambassador Serena Scott of the Intergalactic Council," he told them. "Bylld almost shit himself when she popped up, he thought it was the guys pranking him. Oh, pardon my language, ma'am."

"It's fine," Sarah said. "But what does she want you to do?"

"She wants to send an Intergalactic Brigade to take custody, so he can be tried before the Council," he told her. "Which means he will likely end up in the highest security prison in the galaxy."

Sarah felt hot tears trying to burst from her eyes.

"Sarah," Slade said, sounding concerned.

"I'm relieved," she managed to say, as Zane wrapped a strong arm around her. "It's finally over."

"It will be soon," Slade said. "I'll be testifying for the Council, of course. I was hoping you might be willing as well."

"Of course we will," Zane said. "I can bear witness to what happened in the swamp and Sarah can corroborate that plus speak about the bank robbery."

She nodded, still having a hard time holding back the tears.

"Thank you for everything you've done," Zane told him solemnly.

"Well, your mate paid me good money," Slade said. "And in addition to that, there were several heftier rewards for his various other crimes. I've got enough to buy that pretty piece of land now, and a bit left over, which I thought you all could put aside for the little one."

"Absolutely not," Sarah said. "All I wanted was justice."

"I had a feeling you might say that," Slade said. "So I already put it up at the bank under his name. If he has a problem with that, he can take it up with me himself when he's old enough to talk."

Zane chuckled and Sarah beamed through her tears.

"So, what are you going to do with yourself now?" Zane asked. "Take a little time off to enjoy your land?"

"Oh, no. No rest for the wicked," Slade chuckled. "Matter of fact, I missed some serious action with rustlers up in the highlands while I was wrapped up collecting Cald-well and his crew."

"The highlands?" Zane said. "That's where Odin is."

"And Liberty," Sarah added, suddenly worried for her friend.

"I wasn't there, so I don't know who all was involved," Slade said. "But there's enough action on this frontier moon to keep a marshal busy for a lifetime. Be glad you have a dragon in the family, little lady."

Sarah smiled up at Zane. She was glad.

Lost in his eyes, she was surprised when she looked back to see that Slade had cleaned his plate.

"That was fantastic," he told Zane. "But I've got to fly. Plenty to do today."

"Thank you so much for coming," Sarah told him. "You come see us anytime."

"You two keep feeding me like this, I'll be like a stray prairie-cat - bound to come back every day," Slade teased.

He headed for the door and they followed, Zane clasping arms with him before he stepped outside.

It was a beautiful day, but most days seemed beautiful now, even the cloudiest ones.

"What are you thinking?" Zane asked, wrapping an arm around her shoulders as they watched Slade ride away.

"We have a good friend here now," she said. "I have a mate and a son. And..."

Zane waited, allowing her time to formulate her thought.

"Wherever my daddy is, I think he's probably at peace," she said at last.

"Yes," Zane agreed. "You've seen to that."

"So, I can be at peace now, too," she realized out loud.

"Are you at peace?" Zane asked, concern in his bright blue eyes, as she felt him touch their bond, testing it.

"What do you think?" she asked, allowing herself to picture her own happiness at their colorful days and wild nights.

She felt his electric response back through the bond immediately.

"I think I can't wait for the baby's nap," he growled, pulling her close.

As he kissed her, she felt her own joy and his, weaving them together, lifting them up.

Their life here might be an adventurous one, but the three of them would face their shared challenges together. And that was enough to make the future seem bright as starlight.

***

Thanks for reading Zane!

Are you ready for another romantic Alien Adoption Agency adventure? Then make sure you grab Liberty and Odin's story right away, so you don't miss a beat!

https://www.tashablack.com/alienadoption.html

TASHA BLACK STARTER LIBRARY

Packed with steamy shifters, mischievous magic, billionaire superheroes, and plenty of HEAT, the Tasha Black Starter Library is the perfect way to dive into Tasha's unique brand of Romance with Bite!

Get your FREE books now at tashablack.com!

ABOUT THE AUTHOR

Tasha Black lives in a big old Victorian in a tiny college town. She loves reading anything she can get her hands on, writing paranormal romance, and sipping pumpkin spice lattes.

Get all the latest info, and claim your FREE Tasha Black Starter Library at www.TashaBlack.com

Plus you'll get the chance for sneak peeks of upcoming titles and other cool stuff!

Keep in touch...
www.tashablack.com
authortashablack@gmail.com

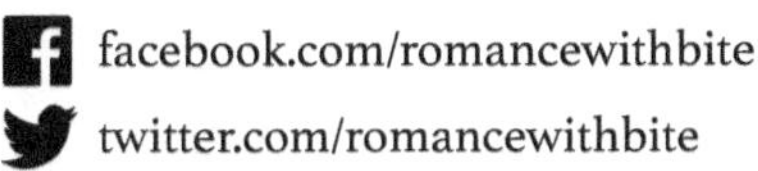

facebook.com/romancewithbite
twitter.com/romancewithbite